She looked at him with an unmistakable intent in her eyes.

"Marcie, this isn't—"

She uttered a sad, small laugh. "Of course it's not a good idea," she murmured, looking up at him. "Right now, I don't care. Do you?"

Joe looked down at her and knew exactly what she was doing.

She wrapped her arms around his neck. He knew her body as well as he knew his own, and he recognized her awakening desire in the suppleness of her muscles, in the softness of her skin and the sultriness in her eyes. He knew, as he always had, on a level much deeper than physical, how much she wanted him.

"No, I don't care," he said, and lowered his mouth to hers.

GONE

—

MALLORY KANE

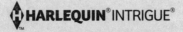

Michael, I love you more than anything.
Congratulations for making it through. We are
going to have so much fun!

Recycling programs
for this product may
not exist in your area.

ISBN-13: 978-0-373-69737-3

GONE

Copyright © 2014 by Rickey R. Mallory

Printed in U.S.A.

www.Harlequin.com

ABOUT THE AUTHOR

Mallory has two very good reasons for loving reading and writing. Her mother was a librarian, and taught her to love and respect books as a precious resource. Her father could hold listeners spellbound for hours with his stories. He was always her biggest fan.

She loves romantic suspense with dangerous heroes and dauntless heroines, and enjoys tossing in a bit of her medical knowledge for an extra dose of intrigue. After twenty-five books published, Mallory is still amazed and thrilled that she actually gets to make up stories for a living.

Mallory lives in Tennessee with her computer-genius husband and three exceptionally intelligent cats. She enjoys hearing from readers. You can write her at mallory@mallorykane.com or via Harlequin.

Books by Mallory Kane

CAST OF CHARACTERS

Joseph Powers—Just about the time Joe Powers finds out he's Con Delancey's son, his estranged wife tells him she's spotted their child, who's been missing for almost two years. Her claim forces him to face his guilt and fear, as well as his still-burning love for his wife. But when the boy is kidnapped because of his relationship to the Delanceys, will Joe lose his son and his wife all over again?

Marcie Powers—Joe's wife has cried wolf twice before, so when she's sure she's seen her son, she knows she can't go to the police. Instead, she goes to Joe, begging him to help her. But before she can convince him that the child really is their missing son, the boy is kidnapped. Has Marcie at last found her child only to lose him forever?

Rhoda Sumner—This childless woman stole little Joshua Powers when his dad set down his baby carrier for a few seconds. Rhoda has never been happier, until the boy's mother spots him in the backseat of her car. Then Rhoda's boyfriend kidnaps the child to get money from the Delanceys. Will she sacrifice her boyfriend to try to keep the child who's not hers?

Howard Lelievre—Howard knows a good thing when he sees it. So when he finds out the kid who Rhoda has shown up with is a Delancey, he kidnaps the child and asks for an outrageous ransom. But he finds out that between the child's parents and Rhoda, he may have bitten off a lot more than he can chew.

Chapter One

There had been a time when just the sight of his wife had Joseph Powers panting with desire. From the blue eyes that sparked fire through his every nerve, to the tips of her pretty pink toes, he'd known, tasted and loved every inch of her. But that was a long time ago, back when they'd been a family, when they'd been happy, when they'd been three. Now, they were just two.

He hadn't seen her in a year, not since the last time she'd called him, crying and begging for his help, promising him that *this* time, unlike every time before, she was sure.

He'd expected her to call, if not today, then tomorrow. Knowing ahead of time didn't make it easier, though. It made it worse. Tomorrow was a big day for both of them. It was her birthday and the second anniversary of their child's disappearance.

He dreaded opening his front door and seeing her standing there, looking sad and lost. Although, she had sounded different this time. Not quite as desperate. Not quite as beaten down. The tone of her voice had given him a tiny scrap of hope. Maybe she'd finally agreed

to take the antidepressants the doctor had prescribed.
Maybe she wanted to see him, not to declare that *this*
time she'd really found Joshua, but to let him know that
she was doing better.

He laughed, a harsh sound that scratched his throat.
Yeah, and pigs can fly.

He paced back and forth, wishing he could wipe
away the memory that haunted him. That split second at
the outdoor market when he'd reached down to pick up
Joshua's baby carrier and encountered empty space. The
helplessness, terror and anger of that horrifying instant
had never faded. Nor had the guilt. They were as strong
and all-consuming as they'd ever been. He'd taken out
a lot of that anger on Marcie, just as she'd taken out her
own sadness, rage and devastating grief on him.

There were some tragedies that were too awful to
share, some burdens that could not be lifted.

The doorbell rang and Joe's heart skipped a beat. He
opened the door and there she was, fresh and beautiful,
her lovely face shiny and clean of makeup. Her beautiful dark hair was caught up in a ponytail and her wide
blue eyes sparkled with unshed tears. No matter what
had happened between them, no matter how impossible
it was for them to live together with the specter of their
missing child between them, he still loved her. He was
still *in love* with her. That had never changed and he
knew it never would.

Marcie looked pretty and sad and yet determined as
she pushed past him into his apartment. He caught a
faint scent of her melon-scented shampoo and his body
responded. So much for not desiring her anymore.

"Marcie," he said with resignation, closing the door and turning to meet her gaze.

"Joe," she said as she glanced around his apartment. Her gaze stopped for an instant on the small framed photo on the kitchen counter. Joe's gaze followed hers automatically, although he knew the photo as well as he knew his own face in the mirror. It was a picture he'd taken of her and Joshua in the hospital, when Joshua was about four hours old. She walked over and picked up the frame, brushing her fingers across the glass, a wan smile on her face. "I saw him, Joe," she said without taking her eyes off the image.

"Marcie, don't—" he began as it occurred to him that she wasn't frantically excited, the way she'd been every other time she'd been *positive* that she'd spotted Joshua.

She touched the image of Joshua's round newborn face one more time, then set the frame down. She straightened, took a deep breath and clasped her shoulder bag more tightly. "I'm not hysterical," she said evenly. "I saw him. It was only a glimpse into the backseat of a car, but I know—" She stopped and pressed her lips together before continuing. "I'm almost positive it was Joshua."

Almost positive? Joe stared at her, trying to reconcile this new Marcie with the hysterical woman who, within the first six months after Joshua was gone, had been *absolutely positive* she'd spotted him at least four times. Who'd screamed and thrown things the first time he'd suggested that she go to a grief counselor. He ran a hand across the back of his neck. "Marcie, are you on medication?"

She rolled her eyes toward the ceiling and shook her head. "No," she said on a sigh, meeting his gaze again.

His wife's eyes were damp with tears, but she wasn't the broken and defeated fragile bird he'd watched her become as weeks stretched into months with no word about their missing child.

"You don't believe me," she said.

"About being on medication?"

"About Joshua."

He winced, the way he did whenever he heard his son's name. "We've gone through this so many times before. You can't keep doing this to yourself. You've got to try to get on with your life—"

"Like you did?" she retorted. "Just presto—" she snapped her fingers "—and it's oh, well, Joshua's gone. Guess I'll go help *other* parents find *their* lost children."

Six months after Joshua had disappeared, Joe had gone back to work, because he couldn't sit at home all day and watch Marcie turn into a depressed recluse. But his lucrative corporate attorney position had felt like a waste of time. So he'd quit and taken a job with the National Center for Missing and Exploited Children. The pay was so low it could almost have been considered volunteer work, but at least he felt he was doing something important. The job was both a blessing and a curse. He helped others search for their missing family members while holding out hope that one day, one of these trails would lead to his own son. Then maybe, no matter what the outcome, he and Marcie could finally get closure.

"Marcie, I've told you before, the fact that I went back to work didn't mean—"

"No," Marcie said, waving a hand dismissively. "I'm not letting myself get sucked into that argument. I came here for one reason and one reason only. I saw our son. I copied down the car's license plate and I need your help."

"You got the license plate number?"

"The woman has our child, Joe."

He steeled himself. So she'd written down a license plate this time. So she was calm—almost too calm, he thought—rather than hysterical. That didn't make her any less delusional. "Come on, Marcie. How good a look did you get? Was it a glance into the backseat at a red light? You can't possibly know for sure that a child you saw for a split second in a dark car is Joshua." He felt the empty hole inside him open up and start bleeding. A familiar stinging began behind his eyes. "Do I have to remind you what the police told us? How slim the chances are of finding him as time goes on?"

"I haven't forgotten a single word the police told us," Marcie said stiffly. "I can't be like you, Joe. I can't convince myself that he's dea-dead, so I can pretend I don't hurt anymore. I *saw* him and this time I have a way to find out who has him and I'm going to do it. If it's not him, then at least I'll *know*."

"What are you planning to do? Not go to the police," Joe said stonily, because he couldn't tell her that he didn't think Joshua was dead. Not all the time. "You burned your bridges there."

He was being unfair, blaming her for crying wolf

one too many times. During those first long weeks, his heart had jumped, too, every time he saw a woman with a baby. Time and again, he'd allowed her to call 911, hoping against all reason that she was right and the child she'd seen really was Joshua.

"I know that," she agreed. "But we don't need the police. You work for NCMEC now. You can run a license plate and find the woman."

"I can't do that. I can't use the center's resources for myself."

"Of course you can. It's what you do! Joshua is a missing child. He's on the register, just like the lost children of the parents you help every day. The only difference is, he's our child, Joe. He's my baby."

With those last three broken words, Marcie's face crumpled and she almost lost it. Almost. He wanted to reach out to her, to hold her and comfort her and, yes, take some comfort himself, but the two of them didn't do that anymore. It had been well over a year since they'd even touched.

As he gaped in stunned silence, she pulled herself together. The only sign of her near breakdown was the two tears that slid slowly down her cheeks.

He turned and headed to the kitchen, muttering something about a glass of water. But truthfully, he needed a moment to think about what she'd said and, yes, to get control of his own emotions.

She was right, of course. Joshua was listed in the National Center for Missing and Exploited Children database. There was no reason he couldn't run the plates. He was reviewing several cold cases in the New Orleans area. Joshua's disappearance could easily be classified as one of those. But as soon as he did, everyone from his staff here in New Orleans, to the employees at the center's headquarters in Virginia, would contact him and want to hear what he'd found out about Joshua that made him start searching again. He didn't want to tell them that once again, on the anniversary of their son's disappearance, his wife had started seeing their child everywhere she went.

He drew a glass of cold water from the refrigerator dispenser and took a long swallow, then wiped his face with a shaking hand. Scowling, he clenched his fist so hard his hand cramped.

He didn't have the strength or the will to get sucked into Marcie's fantasy world again, where Joshua was out there waiting for his mommy and daddy to find him. The sick emptiness inside him started aching and he imagined the taste of blood. After a second cooling swallow for himself, he took the water to Marcie. She refused it, so he set it down on the coffee table.

"Where did you see the car?" he asked.

"I drove up to Hammond yesterday to see my aunt, and when I pulled up to a red light, there was a woman in a Nissan hatchback with a child seat in the back. I eased forward until I could see him." She took a deep breath. "Joe—"

He closed his eyes.

"It was Joshua. I'm not saying I *know* it was him. But I'm almost positive. His face, Joe. That little widow's peak. The woman saw me looking and I swear she went white as a sheet. As soon as the light turned green she gunned her car and sped away. I couldn't keep up with her."

He picked up the water glass and took a sip because he couldn't meet her gaze. The hope in her expression would fuel his, and he knew that one of them had to remain rational. Being the unflappable, levelheaded one had been his job ever since that awful moment in the outdoor market. Yes, he was the rational one. The strong one. Trouble was, he was also the guilty one. It had been his fault that their baby was gone.

"What about the woman?" he asked. "Did you get a good look at her? Could you identify her if you saw her again?"

"Yes," she said, surprising him. "She was probably in her late forties. Her hair had that faded noncolor that blondes get before they go gray. I can't tell you how tall or how large she was, but behind the wheel of the Nissan she looked small and thin. Oh, and she had a scar on her upper lip."

Joe's surprise turned to amazement and worry. Previously when she'd insisted that she'd seen Joshua, her claims were vague and boundless. But today, not only did she have a description of the car and the license plate, but she also had a clear, concise description of the woman. The realization that she'd been thoughtful and careful about getting the information, combined with the mention of Joshua's widow's peak, had Joe's insides churning like an addict looking at a bag of heroin. For Joe, that bag held hope, and for him, hope was a drug that fed on his ability to function.

What could it hurt if he ran the plate at the center?

Maybe it would help Marcie—help them both—if he found out for sure that the child she saw was not Joshua. Even though his conscious mind was certain that this random sighting at a random red light could not possibly be the answer to their prayers, in another, deeper place, far below his conscious mind, a faint thought that was as much feelings as words arose, and it was anything but rational. He did his best to ignore its insidious, hopeful message.

"Maybe I could run that license plate." As soon as he said it he wanted to take it back. If he'd had any sense, he'd have waited until after he'd run it. Then he could have gone to her with a fait accompli. *It's not Joshua. Sorry, hon.*

"Joe? Really?" Her face brightened and her eyes welled with tears again. "Thank you," she whispered, stepping toward him.

It was the most natural thing in the world to open his arms and pull her in. But holding her sent conflicting emotions roiling through his insides. In one sense, it was like coming home. She was his beautiful princess. The girl he'd been in love with ever since they were in high school together. The woman he'd married and promised to love and cherish as long as they lived. The mother of his child.

But as wonderful as it was to hold her, it was even more painful. It reminded him of the countless nights they'd spent huddled together after Joshua had disappeared, clinging to each other as if each one feared the other would disappear. And the equally countless nights when they'd lain back-to-back, rigid and sleepless, but unwilling to offer or ask for help.

A shudder rippled through him as the struggle continued inside him between his need to hold this woman he'd loved as long as he could remember, and his need to protect himself from the painful, heartbreaking memories she'd brought with her.

Her body was lighter, less substantial than he remembered. She'd lost weight in the year since they'd split. He felt bones where before she'd been soft and curvy. He'd already noticed that her face was not just paler, but thinner, as well.

She pressed her temple against the hollow of his throat and he felt her tears dampening his skin. Carefully, he wrapped his arms around her and pressed his nose against her hair, breathing in the evocative scent of her shampoo.

Just a few seconds of comfort, he thought, trying not to notice that her body still fit with his, as though they were two parts of the same whole. "Happy birthday, Marcie," he said tentatively, wondering if mentioning it would cause her to pull away. But she didn't. After a few moments, she lifted her head slightly, causing Joe's nose to press more firmly against her hair. His arms tightened, and when they did, Marcie's fingers curled against his chest. She looked up at him, her eyes no longer wet with tears, but shimmering with something he'd thought was gone forever. His body recognized it, too. He almost groaned aloud as he felt the stirrings of arousal for the first time in a very long time. Gritting his teeth, he wrapped his fingers around her upper arms and set her away from him.

"Joe," she said, her voice low and sultry, a signal—an invitation—that he hadn't heard in two years, but that he'd never before ignored or denied. She looked at him with an unmistakable intent in her eyes.

"Marcie, this isn't—"

She uttered a sad, small laugh. "Of course it's not a good idea," she murmured, looking up at him. "Right now, I don't care. Do you?"

He looked down at her and knew exactly what she was doing. She was seeking a way to push aside the sadness and pain for a while. While it wasn't a good idea, it wasn't the worst thing they could do to each other.

She wrapped her arms around his neck. He knew her body as well as he knew his own and he recognized her awakening desire in the suppleness of her muscles, in the softness of her skin and the smokiness in her eyes. He knew as he always had, on a level much deeper than physical, how much she wanted him. "No, I don't care," he said and lowered his mouth to hers and kissed her.

Once he'd guided her to the bedroom, they came together on his unmade bed with a frenzy that echoed the need and excitement of their first time long ago. They stripped off their clothes without speaking, and Joe pulled her to him. As their bodies melded together like two parts of the same whole, he sighed and heard her quickening breaths echoing his. He was already hard and when Marcie felt him pressed against her, she whispered, "Now, Joe. Now."

"Not yet," he answered, moving his hand down to caress her. To his surprise, she was ready.

"Now," she whispered.

They made love quickly, greedily, like the long-lost lovers they were. It didn't take long for either of them to reach their climax. Once they were done and heaving with exertion and the delicious fatigue of satiation, they still clung to each other.

After their breaths and heartbeats finally returned to normal, she curled up against him, her head in the spot between his chest and shoulder where it fit perfectly. He kissed her languidly then lay beside her, trailing his fingers along her spine. He drifted then woke, then drifted again. Each time he came awake, he found that his fingertips were still lightly caressing her lusciously smooth, firm skin. They dozed.

A long time later, she touched his cheek. "Joe?"

He heard her voice through a pleasant, drowsy haze. "Mmm?" he whispered, not willing to leave his half-asleep world, where dreams and reality swirled, forming a strange, exotic fantasy.

She put her lips close to his ear. "How long will it take you to run the license plate?"

His fantasy world crashed as he jerked awake. "What?" he muttered automatically, although he'd heard her loud and clear. He sat up and reached for his pants, pulling them on without bothering to buckle the belt. Then he turned to her. She was still lying there on her side, but she'd pulled the sheet up to cover herself. "Is that what this was about?" he demanded.

Her eyes widened. Then they slid away from his gaze

to a point somewhere behind him as she sat up, pulling the sheet with her. "No, of course not," she said, sounding hurt. "I shouldn't have said anything. Sorry."

"Don't worry, Marcie. I'll get it, but I don't know what you're going to do with it. You can't take it to the police. This will be the fourth time you've cried wolf."

He pushed his fingers through his hair then wiped a hand down his face. "And when you've got the woman's name, what are you going to do? Scream at her, like you've done before? Try to grab her child?" He laughed, a harsh explosion that hurt his throat. "You're going to end up in prison—or the loony bin."

"Stop it!" Marcie cried. She tossed aside the covers and got out of bed, quickly donning her clothes. "That's not what I meant. I wouldn't do that. I'm sorry! I'm sorry, okay?" She grabbed her shoes and hurried from the bedroom into the living room.

Joe followed her. He didn't know what to say—what to think even. The sex had been mind-blowing, as it always was between them. But had she really done it just to convince him to help her with the license plate? He'd never thought of her as a calculating or manipulative person. But he hadn't seen her in a year.

During that time, she'd somehow managed to pull herself together, which seemed remarkable, given how sad and broken she'd been. What else had she learned in the past year? Was she transforming from grief-stricken mother to levelheaded supermom, resorting to anything, including sexual manipulation, to find her child?

When he stepped into the living room, she was fully dressed. Her hair, which had come out of its ponytail during their lovemaking, was sleek and neat again, and she regarded him with serene composure.

"I apologize, Joe. I didn't—" She stopped and started again. "I'd better be going. When you run the tag, you have my phone number."

"Yeah," he said. He crossed his arms and stood stoically as she left, closing the door behind her. He didn't move until he heard her car start and pull away from the curb. Then he went into the bathroom and splashed cold water on his face.

There for a moment, he'd thought that she'd finally come to terms with their loss. To look at Joshua's disappearance, if not rationally, then at least with less debilitating emotion. She'd finally conquered the frantic desperation that had made her think every toddler she saw was her child.

But now he wasn't so sure. She was a woman even before she was a mother, so maybe she'd done what women did. She'd used sex to get what she'd wanted. If she'd never done it before, maybe it was for the simple reason that in all the years they'd been together she'd never needed to.

So she'd seduced him and, of course, as soon as she beckoned, he'd followed her like a puppy starved for attention. What a stupid jerk he was.

Chapter Two

That night, Marcie couldn't sleep. Every time she managed to drift off, her mind started playing tricks on her. One time she dreamed that she was running after the woman who had Joshua, but the police were chasing her like the Keystone Kops, laughing and pointing and popping up everywhere she turned. The next time she managed to relax, she dreamed of Joe, his strong arms and gentle words surrounding her. But too soon, the Keystone Kops were back and everyone was running in jerky circles like an ancient silent movie on fast-forward.

Finally she got up, exhausted by the disturbing and conflicting dreams, and went to the kitchen for a glass of water.

What had gotten into her, that she'd let herself get caught up in Joe again? Natural, she supposed, given that she'd known and loved him for almost half her life. But just because making love with him had felt natural and familiar and as wildly exciting as ever, it didn't make it a smart thing to do.

His harsh voice echoed in her head. *Is that what this*

was about? His words had sounded angry, but his tone also carried a note of hurt. Well, it had hurt her, too, that he would think that of her.

When he'd agreed to run the license plate, she'd been so grateful, so relieved. Stepping into his arms had felt like coming home. When he'd embraced her and kissed her, she'd been so consumed with desire and love that for those brief moments, the loneliness and grief of the past two years had flown out of her head.

Now, sitting in the big, lonely house they had bought together when they'd found out they were pregnant, she could see it all from Joe's point of view. His, to put it kindly, *unconventional* upbringing had instilled in him a distrust of women that had been a challenge for her from the moment they'd met. Over the years, she'd convinced him that she was nothing like his mother, and they'd had a happy marriage—or so she'd thought.

After Joshua was stolen, Joe's guilt had caused all his trust issues to resurface. Marcie knew that. She also knew that the unbearable pain of losing her baby had made her unfairly cruel and heartless toward him. She'd spent the first heartbreaking months blaming him for Joshua's disappearance. And the awful thing was that he'd accepted all the guilt and blame. He had taken everything she'd dished out.

They'd ended up so far apart that Marcie had been sure nothing could bring them back together. And nothing had. Until today.

She had gone to see him for one reason only. He was her last hope. He'd been right about the police. After she'd cried wolf so many times, they'd never listen to her again. And her friends had either given up on her, or had drifted away into the land of "call me if you need to talk."

Had she made love to him to secure his promise to run the license plate of that car? No, she told herself sternly. Not on any conscious level. It had truly been a sweet and poignant, if frenzied, reunion of long-estranged lovers. She shivered as her body tightened in memory of her explosive climax.

If Joe thought she'd manipulated him, wasn't that his problem, not hers? She'd gotten what she'd needed. His opinion of her was secondary. She'd been terrified that he would refuse to help her, but there had been no mistaking the excitement and hope in his eyes when she'd told him about the license plate and described the woman. He might act as if he were over Joshua, but she was still his wife and she knew him. He was as committed to following up on this crumb of hope as she was.

TUESDAY MORNING, JOE was in his office at the National Center for Missing and Exploited Children. After training and working at the headquarters in Alexandria, Virginia, for six months, he'd secured approval to open a satellite office in New Orleans. He had a small staff and an even smaller budget, but he believed in the center's mission and purpose, and he felt as though he were making up in a small way for the few seconds of inattention that had allowed someone to steal his son from him.

His purpose hadn't been entirely altruistic—maybe not at all. He'd checked the reports and descriptions of rescued children, as well as recovered remains, every

week, scarcely able to breathe until he'd finished reading each one.

He was staring at the computer screen, weighing the
pros and cons of entering his son's name and description
into the NCMEC database, when someone knocked on
the open door. He looked up. It was his mother. Kit Powers had on a short black skirt, a sleek red jacket and red
platform heels. She looked like a million dollars, as she
always did, and years younger than her real age, which
was probably early sixties. It occurred to him that he'd
never known for sure how old she was. "Kit," he said,
rising. "What are you doing here?"

She glanced over her shoulder at Jennie, the young
case-analysis intern who was standing behind her with
an openmouthed stare. "Thank you, sweetheart. I'm
going to tell my son to give you a raise." She looked at
Joe. "Give her a raise, darling. She's adorable."

Jennie blushed a bright pink and backed away.

"Interns don't make any money and *adorable* is not
a job requirement," he said. Why had she told the intern that he was her son? She'd always told him and
his younger brother, Teague, to call her Kit, and she'd
never introduced either of them in any other way than
"and this is Joe," or "this is Teague."

In her day, Kit Powers had been the most famous,
most recognizable exotic dancer in the French Quarter.
Joe knew a lot about his mother's life after he was born,
not so much from her as from the colorful characters
who had been her family, and therefore his. He'd been
babysat by transvestites in sequins and false eyelashes,
street mimes, jazz musicians who let him puff on a joint

when he was too young to fix his own breakfast. And he'd loved them almost as much as he loved Kit.

He knew that, no matter how much she needed money, his mother had never danced nude, but he'd seen photos of the costumes she'd worn. She'd appeared in some of the most beautiful and revealing costumes ever seen outside of Lady Gaga's closet. He also knew that she had a lot of money, probably from her famous lover Con Delancey, because she'd used it to set up very large trusts for Teague and him. Then, when Joshua was born, she'd done the same for him.

"What brings you out to Metairie?" he asked.

"Does a mother need a reason to come and see her son?" She stepped over and turned her cheek for a kiss, then looked around. "I've never seen your offices. Give me the tour."

He gestured around him. "Well, this is *the offices*. And that concludes the tour. Have a seat." He grabbed a stack of books from the only other chair in the room, but she waved a beautifully manicured hand.

"No. I really don't have time. I've got yoga this morning and I'm taking a cake-baking class in the afternoon."

Joe laughed. "You're going to yoga dressed like that?"

"Don't be silly. I have my yoga outfit in here." She indicated the large Coach leather tote over her shoulder.

"Okay. So, what's so important you had to take time out of your busy day to drive all the way out to Metairie?" he asked, smiling.

"It's actually not funny, Joseph. I had a very odd visitor a couple of days ago. Ethan Delancey."

"Delancey?" Joe frowned. He, like most people in New Orleans, knew that Kit Powers had had a long affair with the notorious Louisiana politician Con Delancey. The affair had lasted until Con decided to run for governor two years before his death. Up to that point, neither Con nor Kit had ever tried to hide it, although they'd never flaunted it, either.

Most older folks in the area figured Delancey was entitled, since rumors had flown for years that Lilibelle, Con's wife, had locked her bedroom door after the birth of their third child.

"What did he want?"

Kit glanced around, noticed Joe's diploma and some other framed documents on the wall next to the door and stepped over to examine them. She was stalling, and that wasn't like her.

"Kit, what's wrong?" he asked.

She turned and clasped her hands in front of her. "You read about the murder of Senator Darby Sills, I assume," she said.

"Sure." He frowned at her. She'd never made excuses for her lifestyle, never acted ashamed or guilty about the lovers she took. He and Teague knew men from every walk of life as friends of their mother, although few of them had been more famous or more notorious than Con Delancey. Was Senator Sills one of her conquests? "What about it?"

"Detective Delancey brought me something that was found in Darby Sills's house. He claimed he didn't know how Sills had come across it, but that it appeared to be the only copy."

A bad feeling began in Joe's chest, pressing down, making it hard to breathe. "The only copy of what?"

She dug into the tote and pulled out a thin manila folder that appeared to have only one sheet of paper in it. She handed him the folder and turned to gaze at the framed documents on the wall again.

Joe waited for a few seconds, thinking she'd explain, but she didn't. So he set the folder squarely in front of him on his desk and, after a bit of hesitation, made himself open it. The words he saw at the top of the form added a hundred-pound lead ingot to the weight on his chest.

"What is this?" he asked rhetorically, as his eyes swept down the form and back up. Of course, it was obvious what it was. The question he should have asked rose like a lump in his throat when his gaze landed on a small rectangle toward the top of the page. That tiny area contained a piece of information he had never known, never asked for, never thought he'd wanted.

The form was his birth certificate and in the space for Father was the name Robert Connor Delancey. He swallowed against a lump in his throat, started to speak, failed, cleared his throat and started again. "Is—is this true?" he croaked.

Kit turned around and met his gaze straight on for the first time since she'd come into his office. "Yes," she said. "That's a copy of your official birth certificate."

"Why didn't you—were you ashamed to tell me?"

Her eyes widened with surprise. "No," she said,

shaking her head. "No, darling. Of course not. I loved Con Delancey and he loved me. *And* he loved you."

"Then why didn't you ever tell me?"

"You may not believe me and I know you probably won't understand, but it was out of respect."

"Respect?" he said, cutting her off with a laugh. "For whom? Must be the Delanceys, because *your family* can hardly claim any respect."

His mother drew herself up to her full five feet five inches, tossed her head regally and glared at him. "Joseph, I loved your father. I never wanted to wave my status as *the other woman* in their faces. Con was Catholic and his church was important to him. He would never have gotten a divorce, even if Lilibelle had agreed to give him one, which she wouldn't have."

"How are you such an expert on the Delancey family?" he asked, then answered himself. "Never mind. You were shacking up with the patriarch. Of course you'd know all about them."

"I don't like your tone, young man," Kit snapped.

He had to fight to keep his mouth from turning up in a sneer. "Okay. I'll just have to live with that, because I don't like your lifestyle. Never have. Never will."

Kit Powers drew back her hand as if to slap her son, but he stopped her with a glare. "I'm sorry. I really am. But answer this for me, *Mom*. You made a special trip out here to tell me that Con Delancey is my father? Why now? Why today? I'm thirty years old. Did you not think it could wait another minute?"

His mother's face was pink with frustration and anger. "I'm not sure why you're so upset. I came out here to warn you. Detective Delancey told me that he couldn't guarantee who else saw the birth certificate. He's expecting the information to be leaked to the media, which is why he came to me as soon as he could."

"Wow," Joe said, feeling mean. "I'll be famous." He mimed a newspaper headline. "'Joseph Powers, bastard son of the infamous Con Delancey, let his own son be stolen at a local mall two years ago—'"

"Stop it!" Kit cried. "Stop that right now. You did not *let* him be taken."

"Forget it," he said, tired of the subject and tired of his mother. "I don't care who my father is or was. I never have. Now Teague—he'll get a kick out of being the bastard son of Con Delancey. What did he say?"

"Your brother is not Con Delancey's son," she said flatly.

"He's not?"

She shook her head. "Con left me when he decided to run for governor. I never saw him again. He moved back in with Lilibelle, three years before Teague was born. He was present in your life until you were almost three years old."

"So who *is*—"

"Don't even ask, because I'm not telling you. Either of you. Just let it go."

"So my brother—my *half brother*—doesn't get to know about his dad unless…I guess I should say *until* another Kit Powers scandal occurs? Great job of being a mother, *Kit*."

Her cheeks turned red as she looked at her watch. "I really should be going. My yoga class—"

"Right," Joe said, sitting back down behind his desk. "Well, thanks for the update," he said wryly.

Kit smoothed her skirt and her hair and started to turn toward the doorway.

"Mom?"

"What is it?" she asked, peering at him. "What's wrong?"

"Marcie thinks she saw Joshua."

Kit grimaced. "Oh, Joe." She thought for a couple of seconds. "Yesterday was her birthday, wasn't it? Goodness, has it really been two years? I'm sorry, sweetheart. She still thinks she sees him everywhere?"

Joe shook his head. "No. Until yesterday, I hadn't talked to her or seen her in nearly a year. When she showed up at my door, she seemed different. Not frantic. Not desperate. In fact she sounded pretty rational."

"Is she on medication? Maybe her doctor convinced her to take antidepressants."

He smiled wryly. "No, that's what I thought at first. But however she did it, she seems to have pulled herself together pretty well. She told me she saw a child in a car's backseat and thought it was Joshua. But, Mom, this time she got the car's license plate, and she provided a very good description of the woman driving."

Kit stared at him. "She did? Wow. That's a lot different than the last time."

"She's doing it right this time. She didn't jump out at the red light and scream at the woman to give her back her baby. She didn't scare anyone half to death by stalking them all over the outdoor marketplace. She followed the car, got the license tag and came to see me to see if I could run it for her."

"Joe, you're not buying in to this, are you? I don't think I can stand to see you disappointed again."

"It's a chance, and I can't afford not to take it. But no, I'm not buying in to it again. I'm waiting for the license plate to be run, then I'm going to do a background check on the woman, just like we do any suspected abductor. We check for arrest records, any complaints against them, friends, relatives, church, school, neighborhood. If I can't verify that the child is not Joshua, then we'll make a visit to the woman's house and request a DNA sample. Usually at that point, if the child is an abductee, the abductor's story breaks down. Those are the successful cases."

"And they're what percentage of your entire caseload?" Kit asked, her face suddenly pale and pinched.

"I'm not getting my hopes up, Kit, I promise." *Liar.* Of course he was getting his hopes up. Marcie was almost positive she'd seen their son.

"I have to go," his mother said, still looking as though she'd just heard awful news. She stepped forward and held out her arms for a hug. He got up, bent down and hugged her, accepting her tight, warm embrace in return. "I love you, Joe. You and Marcie. Please don't get yourselves hurt again. When you find out it's not Joshua, be careful. Let Marcie down easily."

"I love you, too, Kit."

She pulled back and looked him square in the eyes. "If you need anything—*anything*—you call me. Understand? And, Joseph, it's about time you started calling me Mom," she admonished.

Before he could think up an answer to that, she'd slipped out the door.

THE PAST TWO YEARS had been the happiest that Rhoda Sumner had ever had in her life. Her little boy was beautiful and perfect. That good-for-nothing mooch Howard, who still claimed he was going to marry her one day *when his ship came in,* spent most of his days over on Bayou Picou, fishing. Rhoda cared about Howard. He brought fish home and cleaned them himself, and he handed over his disability check to her every month. He was happy as a clam to have a woman, a place to live and money for beer and bait. And he never said a word about the kid who'd showed up two years ago. In fact, his usual practice was to pretend the kid didn't exist.

Although Rhoda had never been blessed with a child, she'd told everyone that Joshy was her grandson, and she was rearing him because her daughter couldn't stay off drugs. She took him to Sunday school, bought him clothes at the Walmart in Hammond, and every morning from eight o'clock until ten, she sat him in a little antique wooden school desk she'd found and played educational games with him. He wasn't yet three and he already knew how to count to twenty and identify eight colors. He could get through *P* singing the alphabet song and she was starting to teach him that each letter had a shape and a sound.

"Now which letter is this, Joshy?" she said, holding up a flash card with a *B* on it.

"Bee!" he shouted.

"That's right. You are such a smart boy."

"I a smart boy," he replied and held up three fingers. "I'n three."

"Almost. Now, what letter—?" Before she could finish her sentence, she heard the front door slam. It was Howard. With a sniff of irritation, she got up from the low chair where she sat in front of Joshy.

"Oh, no!" Joshy said. "Howarr. Oh, no. He yells."

"I know, smart boy," Rhoda said to him. "Let's go into your room. I'll turn on the TV for you." She walked with Joshy into his room and turned the TV to a children's channel. "Watch TV while I talk to Howard, okay?"

"Okay, Gramma."

When Rhoda came out of Joshy's room and closed the door, Howard was staring into the open refrigerator door. "Rhoda!" he shouted as she walked into the kitchen.

"I'm right here," she snapped.

"Why isn't there ever anything to eat in here?"

"If I ever knew when you might show up, I could cook something for you."

"Whatcha got?" Howard asked, ignoring her admonishment.

"There's ham and I've got plenty of eggs."

"Got any Tabasco?"

Rhoda laughed. "When have I ever run out of Tabasco?"

Howard grunted. "Eggs and ham and lots of toast."

She sighed. "Want coffee?"

"What do you think?" he grumbled. "Where's the kid?"

That question surprised her. He'd seen her coming out of Joshy's room, so he had to know he was in there. And when had he started acknowledging that the boy even existed? "He's in his room," she said as she grabbed a plate of sliced ham and a carton of eggs out of the refrigerator. "Why?"

Howard just grunted as he sat down at the kitchen table and shook out the newspaper she'd carefully folded and set aside earlier, when she'd finished reading the headlines and the comics. It took her less than ten minutes to fix his breakfast. It took him less than five to wolf it down. He ate and drank his coffee without ever looking up from the paper.

"What are you doing here this time of the morning, Howard?"

"Hungry," he grunted.

"So your whoring ex-girlfriend don't cook?"

He looked at her flatly. "*If* I ever saw my whoring ex-girlfriend that lives over in Killian and has a sugar daddy, she'd probably treat me way better than my *boring* girlfriend."

Rhoda sniffed and nodded. "You're a real comedian, Howard. A real funny guy. I hope you're not planning on sticking around. I've got a lot to do today."

Howard ignored her and kept reading and sipping coffee. After a couple of minutes, he tapped the paper with his forefinger. "Here it is," he muttered, then folded the paper twice and pointed at an article.

"Here's what?" she asked, running water into the

sink and squirting dishwashing liquid into it. Steam rose, mixed with a few stray bubbles that escaped from the hot soapy water. "Is Kroger having a sale?"

"Look at this," he said, tapping the paper again.

"I'm busy."

"Look at it!" he shouted.

Rhoda slung water and soap off her fingers, dried them on her apron and took the paper. She saw an article about a new fishing camp being built near Killian. That was no news. The area was becoming more popular for fishing every year. "What?" she asked. "I don't see anything."

"I don't know how you find your glasses in the morning, woman. Right there in the middle. The column titled Delancey something-or-other."

Rhoda read the short article. Then she read it again, hoping that she'd misread it somehow. But she hadn't. She closed her eyes.

"You're such an idiot, Rho. How in the hell, out of all the kids in all the public places in a city as big as New Orleans, did you manage to grab a Delancey?"

"Wait a minute. We don't know for sure—"

"The hell we don't." Howard hauled his bulk up out of the kitchen chair and walked to the back door and looked out. "You don't think I missed the name and telephone number sewed into that little shirt and taped to the baby carrier, do you?"

Rhoda didn't say anything. She was still staring at the article, although after reading it six times, she could probably recite it by heart.

LOCAL ATTORNEY'S CONNECTION
WITH DELANCEYS SHOCKS
NEW ORLEANS

Papers confiscated during the investigation into
Senator Darby Sills's murder have revealed a star-
tling connection between a local attorney, Joseph
Robert Powers, and the powerful and influential
Delanceys of Chef Voleur and New Orleans, Lou-
isiana. Powers is the son of controversial French
Quarter celebrity Kit Powers, rumored to have
been politician Con Delancey's long-time lover.
A birth certificate confiscated from Sills's house
proves that Joseph Powers is in fact the son of Con
Delancey. The thirty-year-old Powers, who estab-
lished a satellite office of the National Center for
Missing and Exploited Children in New Orleans
after his own son, Joshua Joseph, disappeared in
March of 2012, could not be reached for comment.
A representative for the Delanceys informed us
that they are unaware of any connection and have
never met Powers or his mother.

She'd never talked about where Joshy had come
from, not even to Howard. Not surprisingly, he'd never
asked. Rhoda realized that she'd almost bought in to
her own lie. She'd almost told Howard that the article
couldn't be true because Joshy was her daughter's child.
Her daughter that didn't exist.

But no matter how much Rhoda wanted to deny it,
the fact was, little Joshy, who was her grandson in every

way but flesh and blood, was the son of Joseph Powers and the grandson of Con Delancey. She felt a sinking sensation in her stomach. Nothing good could come of this.

"What do you think of that, Rho?" Howard asked. When she looked at him he was sneering in the way he did when he knew he had the upper hand.

"I'm just going to have to be more careful. I won't take him to Sunday school anymore. After this article, everybody in the state is going to be staring at every child his age, asking themselves if that boy, or that one or that one, could be Con Delancey's grandson."

"You know what?" He thumped the paper. "This gives me an idea."

"What?" Rhoda didn't like the sound of Howard's voice or the look on his face. "What idea could you possibly have that would help anything?"

"Woman, if you'd listen to me for one minute, I'll tell you. That kid is a gold mine. All we gotta do is call the Delanceys and tell them we've got their grandkid and we'll be happy to give him back, for a price."

"No!" Rhoda said, backing toward the hallway to the bedrooms. She wanted to be between Howard and Joshy's room. Not that she could stop Howard if he decided to get to Joshy. "No. He is *not* a gold mine. He is my grandson. He's mine. He's nothing to do with you or them."

"If he's worth money, he's a *lot* to do with me. You know how bad I been wanting to build me a building near a dock where I could make a little money working on boat motors. We could build us a nice house out there on Bayou Picou."

"You listen to me, Howard Lelievre. I know things about you. I know your secrets. You start messing with my little Joshy and I'll get you in so much trouble they'll put you *under* the jail. Do you understand me?"

Howard gaped at her. "Oh, yeah? Are you really that stupid, woman? You know what I can do to you with one hand tied behind my back? You won't be able to tell nobody nothing once I get through with you."

Rhoda laughed. "Big talker. All I need is two seconds to grab my rifle. 'Cause I can put a slug through a rabbit's eye at thirty yards. Your big gigantic head'll be a piece of cake. Actually more like a bowl of pudding, and don't you forget it."

"Hell," he said. "What's the matter with you, woman? All I want to do is fish. And maybe have a little store or bait shop where I can fix motors and stuff. Don't you want enough money so you don't have to worry about anything?"

Not as much as I want that little boy. Rhoda shook her head. "You're an idiot, Howard," she said, pointing her finger at him. "Don't forget what I said. You touch one single hair on that child's head and you'll be answering to *me*."

To her relief, Howard actually looked worried. He shrugged, stuck his thumbs in the shoulder straps of his denim overalls and headed toward the front door. Rhoda heard him cursing under his breath.

"Watch what you say, you foul-mouthed good-for-nothing," she called after him. "Little pitchers have big ears."

His footsteps stopped. "Little pitchers can get *broken,* Rhoda."

Chapter Three

Joe decided not to search for Marcie's license plate using NCMEC resources, if only because it was connected to the New Orleans Police Department's computer system. Now that his parentage was big news on page three of the *Times-Picayune,* he didn't want his name showing up there, especially since there were Delanceys on the police force. So he called up a friend whose mother was a police dispatcher in the Baton Rouge area.

"It's a Livingston Parish tag," Joe told his friend Terry. Within two hours he knew that the vehicle was a 2003 Nissan hatchback, registered to a Hardison Sumner, of Killian, Louisiana.

"Interesting note," Terry said. "Mom tells me that Hardison Sumner is deceased. Apparently it's his wife who's driving it."

"Did Sumner or his wife have a police record?"

"Nothing Mom could chase down. The car is clean, too. No outstanding parking tickets or citations. Say, Joe, I saw the papers the other day. Is everything okay with you—"

Joe cut him off, saying he had to be in court, thanked

him for the information and hung up. He'd decided about three seconds after his mother left yesterday that he wasn't going to answer any questions about his mother, his *alleged* father or himself. He wasn't going to mention it to Marcie, either, if she hadn't read it in the paper already. One personal crisis at a time was all he could handle. Who his father might be meant nothing to him compared to the possibility that following this lead might bring his son back to him.

He drove up to Metairie, to the house where he and Marcie had lived until he'd moved out. He'd needed to separate himself from her sadness and overwhelming grief. But he'd also wanted to save her from the added pain of facing him every day and knowing that his neglect had cost them their child.

As he walked up to the front door, he heard music playing from inside the house. It was Mozart, which surprised him. Marcie only listened to Mozart when she was painting. As far as he knew, she hadn't picked up a paintbrush since Joshua went missing. The fact that she was painting now shattered his heart, because he knew what it meant. She was pinning all her hopes on the license plate.

He knocked, and heard the sound echo through the house. The door's sidelights gave a distorted, beveled-glass view of the large foyer. After a moment, he saw her hurrying toward the door and he could tell by the way she moved that she was barefoot. Without warning, his body tightened and lust stabbed him. He'd always thought she had the prettiest feet he'd ever seen. Watching her skip through the house barefoot had always been a huge turn-on for him. He swallowed hard and took a deep breath as she threw the lock and opened the door.

"Yes?" she said, her ponytail still swinging. "Oh, Joe." Her face brightened and her cheeks turned pink. She smoothed stray hairs back from her face.

Facing her, he realized that despite the allure of her bare feet and the ponytail that revealed her beautiful face, he still resented her for using her body to persuade him.

"What are you doing here? Did you run the plate?"

"Yes," he said ungraciously.

"Well, come in and tell me," she said, standing aside and waving a hand. "I know it was a Livingston Parish plate. Where does the woman live? Did you find out anything about her? Does she have any children?"

Joe edged past her into the foyer of the home he was still paying for. He managed to avoid any physical contact. But he could still smell that damn melon-scented shampoo, mixed with the faint smell of oil paint. No, *resentment* was not the right word for what he felt toward her. He was *angry*.

"I've got the information and I'm going to go out there and speak with her, but, Marcie, this is going to be a bust. You know that, right?" Her face fell and he immediately felt like a heel. Still, confronting the issue now, before he came back to her with the disappointing truth, was better. The longer she lived with the idea that the child she'd seen might be Joshua, the harder it was going to be for her to accept that she was wrong again.

"I'm going with you," she said. "When—"

"Oh, hell, no, you're not," he snapped. "You'll wait right here until I get back."

Her cheeks flamed again but this time it wasn't a pretty little blush. It was the spotty red flare of anger. "I'm the one who saw him. I'm the one who got the plate number. I should get to be there when—"

"I said no!" he thundered.

She froze and stared at him.

"I came here to let you know that I'm going to talk to the woman, not to take you with me. I will come back and tell you what I find out, but you know what the odds are. We've heard the experts talk about that so many times. They've studied—"

"*They* didn't see him. *They* aren't his mother. *They* just compile statistics."

"Hon, it's been two years. Have you considered what the odds are that you would just happen to drive up right next to a car carrying our child?"

"No. I haven't considered the odds and I'm not going to. I don't care what the odds are. They don't matter. What matters is that I saw him and I didn't panic or go off half-cocked. I stayed calm and got the license number and gave it to you. I did everything right."

He felt bad for having yelled at her. "You did do everything right," he said gently. "Now you've asked me to help. I am. I'm going to handle this part of it. I'll come straight back here and tell you what happened."

"No, Joe. I can't just sit here and wait. I want to go. Please. I might be able to get a glimpse of Joshua. I might be able to call out to him—" She paused. "Joe?" she said, a tinge of apprehension in her voice. "Do you think he'll recognize my voice? Or was he too young? Oh, Joe, he's not going to remember us, is he?"

"Stop it, hon," Joe said, catching her arm. "You're getting upset. You can't think about that. If we—*when* we find him, we'll worry about that then. For now I'll take care of everything. I promise."

"Will you at least tell me where he is? Is he in Hammond? Are the people nice? Do they have any other children?"

"Absolutely not. I will not tell you anything else." He stepped toward the door. "I need to go. I have some work to do at the office," he said, but Marcie hadn't stopped staring at him.

"What's wrong?" he asked her.

"You're optimistic, aren't you?" she said as her lip started to quiver. "You're a little bit optimistic that she has Joshua."

He pushed past her without answering, grimacing when his arm brushed the firm softness of her breast. Once he was out the door and about to head down the sidewalk, he turned back. He cleared his throat and kicked a stone away with the toe of his shoe. Then he looked up at her. "Yeah, I guess I am. A little."

ON THE DRIVE out to the town of Killian, on the west side of Lake Maurepas, above New Orleans, Joe wished for companionship. He knew it would have been a disaster to bring Marcie, but her presence would have made the drive less boring and less nerve-wracking. Joe had never realized that something could be both boring and nerve-wracking at the same time. But the anticipation of seeing the woman and the child was torture, even though he didn't believe for one moment that the boy was his Joshua. At least he didn't think he did.

He spent most of the drive going over his plan in his head—once he had a plan. He would ask her if she'd noticed anyone suspicious lurking around her little boy. If she questioned him, he'd try to convince her that he was a government official.

Past Killian's tiny downtown area, the roads became little more than asphalt poured down over old shells and rocks. The asphalt dropped off to nothing at the shoulder, and when he met another vehicle, both of them ended up dangerously close to a small drop-off that was deep enough to bend the driveshaft.

When he found the Sumner house, it was set back off the road with what looked like three feet of crawl space under it. Much taller and it could almost be considered a stilt house. Although the ground around the house was dry and sported some fairly nice-looking grass, Joe knew that the area must flood, or the house wouldn't be built up like that.

He turned on a dirt road that was not more than a dirt path. He drove slowly and carefully, following the deep grooves that looked as though they were made by two vehicles that regularly traveled the area. Then he came upon a white plank house. There was an old green pickup and a Nissan hatchback in the front yard. The license plate of the Nissan matched exactly the number Marcie had given him.

So, this was the Sumner house and the vehicle was the same one that Marcie had seen. Although he knew the information he'd gotten was correct, the idea of being this close to the child who could be his son sent his pulse racing. Even being 99 percent sure that Marcie was wrong didn't stop a small sting of anticipation from pricking his chest and allowing hope to bloom.

The heavy, dreadful emptiness that had weighed on him since the moment he'd looked down to find the baby carrier, which he'd set at his feet, gone, came over him. It couldn't be Joshua. The odds were too high against it.

He eased past the Nissan until he had a good clear view of the front door. He pulled out his cell phone and turned it off. He didn't want anything to distract him.

Then he killed the engine and got out, remaining in the arc of the driver's side door, giving whoever was in the house plenty of time to look him over, check out his car and make up their mind that he was harmless.

He feigned looking around the yard and the house. Lying beside the concrete stoop, in the shade of the house, was a black-and-white spotted hound dog, resting. He wasn't asleep, because Joe had seen his head raise a couple of inches as his car approached. But he'd obviously decided neither the car nor the driver was worth getting up and barking at. Joe hoped the inhabitants of the house thought him as harmless as the hound did.

Still moving slowly, Joe closed the driver's door and walked slowly and deliberately toward the house. He saw a curtain flutter on the front window, then heard footsteps clattering on hardwood and the muffled sound of a female voice. He couldn't tell what she said.

About the time he stepped onto the sidewalk that started from nothing about forty feet from the stoop, the front door swung open and a small, slender woman in jeans and a T-shirt and a long gray braid came out, holding a twenty-two rifle in a way that told Joe she'd shot it before—lots of times before.

"What do you want?" she called out.

"My name is Joe Powers—" he began.

"I didn't ask you who you are. I asked you what do you want!" she yelled, lifting the barrel of the rifle about two inches.

"I'm a caseworker for the state," he said, using generic words that he hoped would sound unthreatening. "I want to talk to you about your child." Joe heard a voice from inside the house. It was a small voice—a child's voice, muffled by distance and the screen door. There was no way he could recognize it, or even tell if it were a little girl or a little boy. His heart began pounding so loudly that he wanted to muffle it with his palm.

"Hush, honey," the woman said, her tone kind and indulgent. "Go back to your room."

The child protested.

"No!" the woman said. "Go to your room." She lifted the rifle's barrel another two inches. "Now, you," she said to Joe. "Caseworker for what?"

"Ma'am. I wanted to ask you if you've seen anyone suspicious hanging around you or any friends of yours who have small children. It could happen close to home or when you're out shopping."

"Suspicious? The only suspicious person I see is you. What are you? A cop?"

Joe shook his head and spread his hands, palms out. "No, ma'am. I am not."

"Step out of the shade so I can get a look at you."

"May I just come inside for a minute?" Joe asked, not moving.

"Hell, no, you can't. Don't come any closer. Step sideways."

He stepped out of the shadow of a big pine tree that smelled like turpentine. "There," he said. "Ma'am, we're concerned about a man who has been reported at several malls and near some houses, watching women with small children."

"Shut up a minute," the woman commanded him. "Let me get a look at you."

Joe waited.

"Whereabouts?" she said as she lifted one hand to shade her eyes.

"Excuse me?" Joe asked. He'd heard what she said, but he needed a couple of seconds to sort out what she meant. He finally got that she was talking about where the suspicious character had been spotted. "In Hammond."

"What'd you say your name was?" she cried out, taking hold of the rifle with both hands again. "Where are you from?"

"I'll be happy to explain everything to you once we get inside. I'd like you to look at some pictures." Joe was afraid he was losing her. Was she more interested in him than in the safety of her child, or—?

Suddenly, with a pang in his stomach that felt like an ulcer, he knew why she was questioning him. A picture had been included with the article that had run in the *Times-Picayune*. It wasn't a good one, and it was a few years old, but still, he'd been recognizable.

Joe made a show of looking at his watch. "I'm afraid I've taken up too much of your time, ma'am. I probably ought to go. I've got other people to see. I appreciate you letting me talk to you."

"Gramma?"

There was the voice again. And unless he was horribly mistaken, the voice had said *Gramma*.

The woman's head snapped around toward the inside of the house. "What did I tell you, J—?" She cut herself off abruptly but Joe hadn't missed that she'd almost slipped and said the child's name. It started with a *J*.

His heart kicked into overdrive and his eyes began to sting.

"Gramma," the child called again, and Joe saw the screen door start to open. He strained to catch a glimpse of the child whose small fingers were reaching around the edge of the door, but Ms. Sumner glanced backward. "If you don't mind me right now, I will tan your hide! Now go to your room." She raised her rifle to her shoulder and sighted down the barrel. "And if you don't get out of here, I'm gonna shoot out your tires and then I'm going to shoot you. Coming around here making up stories to get inside my house. Now, you got to the count of three to get in that car and go! And don't you ever come back here!" She raised the gun to her shoulder. "One. Two—"

She fired. The bullet plowed a furrow in the dried

mud and bruised grass stems just to the right of Joe's feet. He jumped and ducked automatically.

"Hah! I aimed to miss that time, but I won't again!"

"Rhoda!" A booming voice came from somewhere to the left and behind the house. Joe heard heavy boots clomping and within seconds, a big, burly man appeared. He was dressed in denim overalls over a faded red T-shirt and he had a fishing rod in one hand and a tackle box in the other. When he saw Rhoda holding the rifle, he slowed down. "Are you all right, woman? What's going on?"

Rhoda whirled to look at the man and Joe took that as his cue to get out. He opened the driver's side door of his car.

"Look at him, Howard!" Rhoda shouted, turning the gun back toward Joe. "Don't he look familiar?"

Joe stood behind the open car door, using it as a shield in case the woman did decide to shoot again.

The burly fisherman spotted him and changed direction. "Hey! What the hell are you doing here? Ain't you got sense enough to get when a woman holding a gun tells you to get?" The man didn't move fast, but he lumbered along at a steady pace.

"Howard, don't scare him to death. *Look* at him!"

Joe glanced toward Ms. Sumner, who had angled her head and was sighting down the barrel again. He imagined he could see right down the inside of the barrel.

"Hey," Howard said. "I know you. You're that lawyer—"

Joe jumped into the driver's seat and cranked the engine. Rhoda fired again. And again, Joe's knee-jerk reaction was to duck. But this time he didn't hear the bullet. It must have passed just above or to the side of the car. He puffed his cheeks and blew out a breath of relief as he threw the transmission into Reverse and backed around in a semicircle, then took off, spinning his wheels and spraying mud and dirt everywhere. The deep tire grooves rocked him back and forth as he sped away, not taking the time to follow the trenches, just wanting to get out of there as fast as he could, hopefully without getting shot.

He heard two more rifle shots in quick succession. He winced and bunched his shoulders. When a beat passed and he didn't hear safety glass pop or feel anything slam into him, he relaxed a little. The base of his spine tingled at the imagined feel of a bullet striking him in the back. He gunned the accelerator and aimed the car for the curve up ahead that would put him out of sight and hopefully out of range of the woman's rifle.

Joe took the curve on two wheels and didn't slow down until he saw the city limits sign for Killian. He slowed to match the town's speed limit. After a couple of moments his brain calmed down enough to concentrate on something other than getting away from the gunfire.

He'd heard a child inside Rhoda Sumner's house. From the timbre of the voice, Joe figured it had to be about two or three years old. A toddler the age Joshua would be now. And she had almost said a name that started with a *J.*

Joe kept his fists white-knuckled on the steering wheel until he was several miles past Killian, then he pulled carefully onto the shoulder of the road and cut his engine. For a long time, he sat there, overwhelmed by all the emotions churning inside him. To his surprise and dismay, he felt a stinging in his eyes and a tightening in his throat. He hadn't cried since he was a kid—a little kid. He'd wanted to. There had been times as he'd held Marcie while she sobbed, that he'd wanted to bury his head in that soft, beautiful curve between her shoulder and neck and cry until the pain inside him subsided. But he never had. Not once.

Now, though, alone in his car, answerable to nobody, responsible for no one, he wept. The tears scalded his cheeks. The sobs made his chest and throat sore. The opposing forces of pain and hope nearly tore him apart.

The sun was going down when he finally wiped his face on his shirtsleeve and started the engine. At the first gas station he came to, he splashed cold water on his face and swore to himself that he would never cry again. He didn't know how women cried so much without it killing them.

As he drove back to Marcie's house, he thought about what he was going to tell her. He couldn't tell her that the man and woman had seen his photo and the scandalous article in the newspaper. If Rhoda and Howard had not already known whose child they'd stolen, they certainly knew now.

There was no way he could explain to her that because he'd driven out there, he'd confirmed for them that the child they had abducted two years ago was a Delancey.

And he sure couldn't tell her that he was convinced

that he'd found their son. After two years of not knowing whether his child was alive or dead, he'd found him.

Joe didn't know what Rhoda and Howard were going to do, but he did know one thing. In finding Joshua, he'd placed him in grave danger.

Chapter Four

Marcie looked at her watch. It was getting dark and she hadn't heard from Joe. She couldn't wait to hear what he'd found out. It still rankled that he'd refused to let her go with him. She was Joshua's mother. She had a perfect right to be there when he confronted the woman.

And she had a right to know where he was and how much longer it was going to take him to get home. Just as she started toward her purse to retrieve her cell phone, the landline rang. She picked it up on the second ring. Almost before she got the word *hello* out of her mouth, a deep, gruff voice said, "I know who you are, and I know who your husband is."

Disgusted, Marcie started to hang up.

"Mrs. Powers, do you want your kid back?"

Her hand froze in midair, stunned by what the awful voice was saying. She brought the phone back to her ear. "Wh-what did you say?" she asked through lips numb with shock.

"You heard me. Now you just listen and listen good. I'm going to call you back tomorrow and tell you what I want you to do. You got that?"

"Who is this?" Marcie demanded, putting all the steel she had into her voice.

He laughed. "Who am I? Why don't you ask your husband? Now you sit tight and don't tell nobody nothing. *Nobody!* Otherwise I'll have to send you a little present. How would you like to get one of your precious kid's fingers in a pretty box?"

Marcie gasped and her stomach turned over. "No! Please. I won't…say anything. Don't hurt him. I swear I won't tell. But where is he? How—"

"Shut! Up!" the man shouted. "Shut up! No questions. Don't talk or you'll get his finger in a pretty box."

She heard a click and the phone went dead.

Marcie stared at the words displayed on the tiny screen. *Out of area.* Her stomach cramped and her saliva turned acrid. She rushed to the sink and splashed cold water on her face, willing it to wash away the image of her precious baby's bloody finger in a box. She sucked in a mouthful of water, hoping the coolness would settle her stomach.

Was this her fault? Had the woman in the car known her? Known she was Joshua's real mother? That meant the little boy she'd seen really was hers. But it also meant she may have put his life in danger. Her baby! Her son! He was out there with a dangerous, violent man. Waiting for her to find him.

She didn't know how long she'd been sitting there at the kitchen counter when she finally heard a car pull up outside and cut its engine. When she straightened, she felt a twinge in her back. She hurried to the foyer and peered through the sidelights. It was Joe. Her knees literally went weak. She flung open the door and threw herself into his arms, almost knocking him over.

"Hey, Marcie, what—?"

"Joe! Somebody called!" she cried, pushing him away to look at him, then hugging him again. "I'm so scared. I don't know what to do!"

He gripped her upper arms and set her far enough away from him that he could see her face. "Tell me," he said. "Who was it?"

"It was a man. He said he had Joshua. He said not to tell anyone, that he'd—" Her breath hitched in a sob. She swallowed and went on. "He'd cut Joshua's finger off and send it to—"

"Marcie," Joe said sharply. "Calm down. I can't understand half of what you're saying. Who called? He said he had Joshua?"

Marcie took a deep breath, hearing it catch at the top like a sob. "I'm—I'm trying to tell you—"

"Marcie, breathe. Take deep, slow breaths. In and out. In and out."

He was talking to her like he had in the breathing classes while she was pregnant. His soothing voice acted on her like a tranquilizer. She breathed in and out, slowly, deeply.

"Now," he said, putting an arm around her and leading her to the couch. "Sit down and tell me exactly what the man said."

She nodded and took one more deep breath for good measure. "He said not to tell anyone or he'd—" She swallowed and took another long, slow breath. "He'd cut

off Joshua's finger and send it to me in a pretty…box."
She felt nauseated again, and out of breath. "Oh, Joe—"

"Shh," Joe said, pulling her to him and rubbing his
palm gently up and down her arm. "It's going to be
okay. That ugly bottom-feeder's not going to do that to
our son. He's a coward and a bully, hiding behind a little
boy. Don't worry. It's going to be all right."

Marcie closed her eyes and let herself be comforted
by him. She loved the feel of his strong chest against
her cheek, loved the soft caress of his hand on her arm.
She wished she could stay right where she was, not
thinking, not feeling anything except the comfort of
Joe's big, strong body surrounding her, protecting her.

But she'd seen the look on his face. The shock—
and the guilt. It was an expression she knew very well.
"Just a minute," she said, thinking of the man's terri-
fying words. "When I asked him who he was, he said
for me to ask you. What did he mean by that?" She
lifted her head from his chest. "Did you see him? Did
he have Joshua?"

Joe didn't answer.

"You *did!* That was him on the phone, wasn't it?" She
frowned. "You know who he is, don't you?"

Then suddenly, it all made sense. Joe had gone out to
that woman's home and questioned her about the child
and now a man was calling, wanting money for her little boy. "Oh, my God, it's not my fault. It's yours! You
saw Joshua, didn't you? I was right. The woman in the
Nissan has Joshua and now he's in danger because you
went out there. Is that man her husband?"

Joe knew exactly what had happened. Rhoda and

the man had recognized him as the bastard Delancey son in the newspaper article. With a sigh, he realized he had to tell Marcy everything.

"Okay, hon, I need you to calm down and listen to me. I think Rhoda—the woman driving the Nissan," he added when he saw her puzzled expression, "took Joshua because she wanted a child. But while I was trying to talk to her, a man showed up in a dirty T-shirt and overalls, carrying a fishing rod. He figured out that I was the father of Rhoda's child right away."

"How? How did he figure it out? What did you tell him?"

He didn't answer her directly. "Listen to me, hon, and stay strong, okay?"

Her eyes grew wide and haunted. "Stay—? What? Oh, my God, what's wrong?"

Joe rubbed his palms up and down her arms. "I think he's planning to try and get money from us."

"Money? Like—like a ransom?" Her expression turned to horror. "They're holding my baby for *ransom?* Why? Why now? That doesn't make sense. They've had him for two years."

Joe shook his head. Suddenly, he couldn't go any further. He couldn't tell her that Rhoda and Howard had decided to hold their child for ransom because he was a Delancey.

"What are we going to do? We don't have any money."

"No, we don't," Joe said, *but the Delanceys do*.

"What are we going to do?"

"Right now, I'm afraid we're going to have to wait for Howard to call back."

JOE WOKE UP, breathing in the faint, fresh air of the home where he and Marcie had been so happy for so long. Before he opened his eyes, he lay still, letting the scents of fresh linens, baby powder and a hint of vanilla wash over him. The poignant memories evoked by the mingled odors brought a lump to the back of his throat.

He shifted and opened his eyes. The first thing he saw was the black-button gaze of a stuffed panda bear. The bear sat in a tiny rocking chair next to the antique crib that had belonged to Marcie's grandmother. In his throat the lump grew, nearly cutting off his breath. He'd slept in the nursery. It hadn't been much of a problem last night. He'd turned out the light as he'd entered the room. Marcie had already converted the couch into a bed and made it up, so all he had to do was undress and climb under the covers. He'd deliberately avoided looking at anything in the room.

Now, in the bright light of morning, he couldn't ignore the baby toys, baby furniture, blue curtains and mobiles hanging over the crib. With the empty place inside him throbbing with grief for his son, he vaulted up off the hide-a-bed sofa, grabbed his slacks and slipped across the hall to the bathroom.

The hot shower eased the pain inside him and soothed the stinging in his eyes. When he stepped out of the stall and reached for a towel, he noticed a neatly folded pair of blue boxers and a white T-shirt. They hadn't been there when he'd started his shower. Gratefully, he donned the clean clothes, pulled on his jeans and headed downstairs to the kitchen.

Marcie was already there, making the coffee. As he

walked in, she finished pouring water into the coffeepot and turned it on. Her hair was damp and pulled back in a high ponytail that made her look like a college kid. But when she turned and looked at him, her eyes were rimmed with red and her nostrils and the corners of her mouth were pinched. She looked awful. Still beautiful, but awful nonetheless.

"Morning," he said.

She didn't answer him. She turned her attention back to the sink, rinsing glasses and placing them in the dishwasher. She dried her hands. Joe noticed that she'd been chewing on her fingernails.

"Marcie, don't you have some of the tranqs the doctor gave you? You ought to be taking them." He took her hand in his and rubbed his thumb across the ragged nails. "You're a nervous wreck."

She jerked her hand away and glared at him. "Thank you, *doctor*. But I don't want to be tranquilized. That man is going to call this morning. What good will I be if I'm drugged?"

He nodded. He understood. It just hurt him to see her hurting so badly. The coffeemaker grumbled and gurgled, announcing that the coffee was ready. She poured herself a cup and took it to the kitchen table and spooned sugar into it.

"Still like a little coffee with your sugar?" Joe said, hoping to make her smile, even if just a little.

He was rewarded with a wan upturn of her lips as she lifted the spoon and inspected it for lingering granules of sugar. She touched the spoon, wiping sugar onto her fingertip. "I'd let Joshua suck a little sugar off my fingertip. He loved—" She set the spoon down with a clatter and lifted the cup to her lips.

Joe poured himself a mugful and sat down beside her. He drank his black. He took a long swallow, regarding her over the rim of his mug as she sipped at hers.

"What happened to us?" she asked.

"What do you mean?" Joe asked, looking at the dark liquid in his mug, then picking it up and sipping.

"Just what I said. What happened?"

He set his mug down a little too hard. "You couldn't—or wouldn't—understand why I went back to work instead of sitting around here and moping, or going over to haunt the outdoor market in case someone showed up with a child, so you could get all excited for two minutes until you got a good look at them."

She shook her head, a pained expression on her face. When she set her cup down, a little bit of coffee sloshed out. "That's not what I'm talking about. I mean before— before Joshua. We weren't good for each other anymore. You were working ten- to twelve-hour days and I spent most of my time painting. I was usually in bed asleep by the time you got home. And you still managed to be jealous of me. You could never believe that I wasn't like your mother. I wasn't then and I'm not now."

He didn't say anything. He knew she was right about what their life had turned into before they got pregnant. But why in hell was she bringing all that up now? It was old news.

"What are you doing, Marcie? Do you really want to talk about that now? I think there are bigger issues here."

She shrugged. "I was so naive. I thought that having a baby would change things. I thought it would make you happy. Make you realize that I wasn't like your mother."

"Don't bring Kit into this," he snapped, a harsh, jagged panic ripping into his chest. He didn't want to talk about his mother. He didn't even want to think about her and the news she'd driven out to Metairie to tell him—was that just three days ago? He didn't want to have to explain to Marcie about the exposé in the newspaper that had prompted Howard to hold Joshua for ransom. He knew she'd have to know eventually, but he was in no hurry to spill this latest chapter in the story of his, as she always put it, *unconventional* upbringing.

"You never want to talk about her. It's like she's some kind of goddess on a pedestal, and you're her guardian." Marcie stood and grabbed her cup to take to the sink. It clattered noisily when she set it down. "What I never could understand is why you never thought about Joshua or me in the same way. Why couldn't you have appointed yourself *guardian* for your child? Maybe if you had—"

Joe stood so abruptly that he knocked the kitchen chair over. "Don't do this. Don't start with me now about letting him be taken."

Marcie turned on him, her electric blue eyes blazing. "But that's exactly what you did. You let him out of your sight. You set his carrier down on the ground. He was your baby and you let him—"

"Stop it!" Joe shouted, clenching his fists at his side.

"You don't have to keep hammering at me! I know! I know what I did! So shut—"

The harsh jangling of the phone made Joe swallow his words. He jumped and whirled toward the sound.

Marcie jumped, too, and let out a little screech of surprise. Then she pressed a hand against her chest. "Oh! It's him," she gasped. "It's him, isn't it? I don't—should I—"

Joe held up a hand that shook. "I'll get it," he said breathlessly. He was terrified. What would Howard demand in return for their child? Would he really hurt Joshua if they couldn't get the money he wanted? "I'll talk to him."

"Joe Powers," he said into the mouthpiece, noticing that the number was blocked.

"Ho-ho! It's you," the guttural voice said. "Did you get a look at your kid yesterday? I hope so because that just might be the last time you ever see him, if you don't do exactly what I say."

Joe glanced at Marcie, who was still standing by the sink. Her hands were clasped in front of her as if in prayer and she was watching him unblinkingly. Joe didn't like what he was about to do, and he knew Marcie wouldn't like it, but it was the only way he could keep the upper hand against this man who was at best a low-life opportunist, and at worst a psychopath. He hadn't worked any kidnappings with NCMEC, but he'd gotten some training from the FBI on handling abductions across state lines. The training plus common sense dictated that he couldn't let Howard get an advantage. Showing weakness could cause harm to the child.

"Hey," Howard said. "Are you listening to me? I said—"

"I heard what you said," Joe replied. "But I'm not interested." Out of the corner of his eye he saw Marcie start, then put her hands over her mouth. He held up his hand, palm out, hoping she understood the message. *Don't worry. I'm handling this. Stay calm.*

Before the other man could speak, Joe went on. "I don't even know if that's my kid. Can you prove that the child is even mine?"

"Joe!" Marcie gasped, starting toward him.

He held up his hand again, then turned his back on her and walked across the room.

"Wha—?" Howard exclaimed, apparently not prepared for that answer. "Of course he's yours, you stupid ass. The same day the newspaper said you lost your child, that's the day my girlfriend showed up with him."

"I'm going to need more than just your word on that, *Howard.* I need proof. Send me a picture of him and a picture of the clothes he was wearing when Rhoda took him." Joe felt Marcie's hand on his arm. He gave a quick shake of his head and touched his lips with his forefinger. "There was a label in his shirt. I want to see that before I talk to you any more."

"Wait!" Howard yelled. "Wait! How do I send it? You want that from me, you gotta give me your cell or your email."

Joe gave him his cell number. "Now you listen to me. If I don't see the pictures in one hour, don't even bother calling." And with that, he hung up. His hand shook as he cradled the phone. He closed his eyes. When he took a deep breath, it caught in his throat and he had to cough.

"Joe, what are you doing? What if they don't call back?" Tears were rolling down Marcie's cheeks. She squeezed the sleeve of his T-shirt in her fist. "Oh, my God! He was so close and now he may be gone again."

"Listen to me, Marcie," Joe said, turning and catching her by the arms. "We've got to keep the upper hand. That's the first thing they teach you at the center. If you show weakness, then they might hurt the child."

"But you just— What if they didn't save the shirt?"

"Then they'll tell us that. Trust me, hon. I know what I'm doing." He thought about his connection with the Delanceys. About how Rhoda and Howard had seen the newspaper article and were now angling for some of the Delancey money. He knew Howard would send the pictures.

What he didn't know was whether he and Marcie would recognize Joshua, who was now twenty months older than they'd last seen.

LOOKING SHELL-SHOCKED AND bewildered, Marcie went upstairs to dress and Joe called his office and talked to his senior caseworker, Valerie. "I won't be in today or Friday. I'll be doing some work from home," he told her.

"Good," she said, before he even finished the sentence. "There are reporters hanging around outside the office like vultures. I'll be thrilled to tell them that you aren't coming in."

"Reporters?" he said. "Are you kidding me?"

"I wish. They're stopping everybody, wanting to

know what we know about you and the Delanceys. Luckily, our staff and interns have enough sense not to answer. We're behind you all the way."

"Tell everybody I appreciate it," he said.

"Joe? Are you all right? You sound terrible."

"I'm fine, Val. Just trying to get everything sorted out. Don't answer any questions, and let everybody know that when all this settles down, we'll have a big celebration. We'll all go out to dinner, on me."

"I'll tell them."

"Thanks. I'm going to sign on from home and run some leads I've been working on for a couple of cold cases," he said. "What's the password for today?"

Valerie gave him the day's password and they hung up. He headed into the small room off the dining room that they'd set up as his home office.

Marcie came downstairs about the time the computer was booting up. "What are you doing?" she asked.

"I'm going to see what I can find out about Howard without having to go into the office," he said. "What about you?"

She shrugged. "Clean up the kitchen. I don't know. Maybe I'll try to read." She wrung her hands helplessly. "I don't know if I can stand this. How long do you think it's going to take for him to call back?"

"I don't know, hon. I'm thinking he'll call as soon as he can get the pictures. He's going to have a problem with Rhoda. She's not going to want to give the boy back. It's obvious that the reason she took him in the first place was to have a child of her own. When he comes to her wanting to take a picture and she finds out his harebrained scheme, she's liable to take—" He stopped, realizing where his thoughts were taking him, but he'd already said too much. Marcie's sharp eyes met his and he knew that she knew exactly where his thoughts were heading.

"She's going to take Joshua and run. Oh, my God, Joe, we've got to stop her."

He did his best to calm her down, but his careless words had started him thinking, too. She was right. The woman just might take the child and leave. She could have relatives anywhere. "This is her home. She's not likely to just pull up roots and head off to parts unknown."

"I would," Marcie said. "If it meant keeping my child safe. I'd do that—I'd travel to the ends of the earth."

Joe nodded. She was right. He'd do the same thing to protect his child, or Marcie.

"We've got to go out there. We've got to talk to her, reason with her, before that man gets his hands on our child." Marcie wrung her hands, then rubbed her temples. "We've got to go now."

Chapter Five

They forwarded the home phone to Joe's cell and headed northwest to Killian. They made it in just under an hour. As the car rounded a curve and the house came into sight, Joe muttered a curse under his breath.

"What is it?" Marcie asked. She'd held on to the grab bar the entire trip. When she let go, her fingers cramped. "What's wrong?"

Joe pulled up near the sidewalk that led up to the wooden front stoop of the house and stopped. He put the car into Park, and left it running. "Wait here," he said.

Marcie grabbed at his arm, latching on to his rolled-up shirtsleeve. "Tell me what's wrong. I'm tired of you ignoring me and refusing to answer my questions."

"When have I—?"

"Joe!"

He settled back down in the driver's seat and looked at her sidelong. "The Nissan was parked out here in front of the house yesterday beside a beat-up green truck."

"Oh," she said, then, *"Oh."* She squinted at the house and the yard, trying to see if there were any signs of the car being driven around to the back. But there were no tire tracks in the yard, or anywhere that she could see, except for the dirt road and the space where Joe had pulled in.

"So you think they're gone?" Her voice tried to quit on her, so great was her fear that they'd fled with her child.

Joe nodded grimly. "It looks like it." He shifted, preparing to climb out of the driver's seat.

Disappointment settled like a stone in her stomach. "I'm going with you," Marcie said, steeling herself for an argument, but to her surprise, Joe didn't say anything. He just reached back inside the car, cut the engine and removed the key.

"Watch your step," he said as they started up the sidewalk to the stoop.

"Did you go inside when you were here before?" she asked.

He shook his head with a wry smile. "Didn't get the chance."

"What did you do?"

"I parked there, just about exactly where the car is now, and I stood by the driver's side door. Rhoda was on the porch there, with a rifle."

Marcie gasped in surprise. "A rifle? Joe, she didn't shoot at you, did she?"

"Three times, I think. Maybe four."

Marcie felt like a bullet had just slammed into her own chest. She pressed a hand against her hammering heart. "Joe!"

"Once while I was standing there at the car door, and then at least twice more as I drove away."

"You could have been killed!"

He made a dismissive gesture. "I got the definite feeling that if Rhoda had wanted to wound or kill me, she'd have done it. Nah. She was making a point with those shots," he said as they reached the porch. He stopped her with a hand on her arm. "Wait here," he murmured.

"No—"

"Marcie, I don't think there's anybody here, but I want to make sure," he muttered sharply. "Here are the keys. If I yell, run back to the car and get out of here."

"I'm not going to leave you here alone," she said, refusing to take the keys.

He grabbed her hand and pressed the key ring into it. "Neither one of us is going another step until you promise me you'll do what I say. I can take care of myself, but Howard is a big man. If he grabs you, we're sunk."

She took the keys, glaring at him. "Fine. I'll just leave you to your fate."

He gave her a crooked smile and nodded. "Good. Now wait here."

She listened, not breathing, but didn't hear anything except his footsteps on hardwood. After about thirty seconds, he opened the screen door and came out onto the porch stoop.

"There's nobody in there. Let's go," he said, looking at his feet as he stepped onto the porch and cupped her elbow in his hand. "Come on."

"Wait a minute. I want to see inside. There might be a clue to where they went."

"I already looked. I didn't see anything."

"Joe, wait. Did you check to see if their luggage is gone? If their toothbrushes are still in the bathroom? They could have just gone shopping or to a movie. We could wait for them."

"What are you going to say?" he asked harshly. "'Hi there. Enjoy the movie? Great. Now give me my son.'"

Marcie glared at him. "What were you going to say?" she blustered back at him.

He winced. "To tell you the truth, I don't know. Now come on. All the more reason to get out of here in case they do come back."

"No," she said. "I want to go inside."

"I'm tired of arguing, Marcie. I told you there's nothing to see." He started down the two steps to the sidewalk, but she didn't move. He pointed to the west. "Howard came from that direction. He had a fishing pole. I doubt there's anything over there but docks and maybe a bait shop, but we could drive that way and see. Ask if anybody knows where they are."

She ignored him and turned toward the door.

He caught her shoulder and when she looked back, his expression was grim. "Marcie, don't."

"Why not? You said there was nobody in there. Is there…blood or something?" Her gaze widened and fear sharpened their blue depths.

"No, hon, nothing like that."

She shrugged, trying to remove his hand. "Then I don't see why I can't go in."

He sniffed, then let her go. "Okay. Go ahead."

Wondering at the defeated note in his voice, she opened the screen door and stepped into the cool, dim house. It took a moment for her eyes to adjust, after being in the bright sunlight. When they did, the first thing she saw was a small wooden table and two chairs. There were blocks and flash cards on the table and right beside it was a whiteboard with two words written on it in box letters. *JOSHY*. Underneath the name was the word *BOY*.

Marcie stared, uncomprehending for a few seconds. Then slowly, as if she were drugged or sick or had just landed on an alien planet, she began to make sense of the things she saw. A groan erupted from her throat and she sank to her knees next to the little table. This was what Joe hadn't wanted her to see. He'd known how much it would upset her. Tears welled in her eyes. She groped blindly on the table and her hand encountered a square, plastic building block. She held on to it as if it were a lifeline.

"He's two years old, almost two and a half," she murmured. "He's learning his *ABC*s—" She gestured vaguely toward the board. "Even words," she said, almost choking.

"I know, hon." She couldn't pinpoint where Joe's voice came from but his words were as hoarse and strained as hers. She felt his hand on her arm and she let him help her to her feet.

She turned to him, proffering the block, her lower lip trembling with the effort not to cry. He ignored the plastic cube and just pulled her close. But she didn't—

she couldn't—let him hold her right now. Hunching her shoulders, she stepped around him and went into the small kitchen. Beside the sink were several sippy cups turned upside down on a towel. An empty carton of juice was in the trash can.

Marcie felt as though she were choking and smothering. No matter how hard she tried, she couldn't get a full breath.

"Just breathe," Joe said softly in her ear. She hadn't heard him come up beside her. "Just breathe, slowly, evenly. You'll be okay."

She did what he told her to, because she had no choice. She was hyperventilating. She knew that. But she couldn't stop it without Joe's help. How many times had it happened since Joshua had disappeared? Five? Ten?

"Breathe evenly," he kept repeating. "Slowly."

Finally she could take a full breath without it hitching. "Okay," she said, a little breathlessly. "It's okay now."

"Come on, let's go outside." He took the block from her and bent to set it back down on the little table.

"No!" she cried, reaching for it. "I want to keep it."

"I don't see why—"

"Give it to me."

Joe gave her the block.

She held it in both hands, pressed against her chest. "She was teaching him, Joe. She was teaching my little boy. Look at the block. It has a *J* on it. Did you see the kitchen?"

He didn't speak. He just waited for her to finish.

"She took care of him. She gave him juice. Bought him little cups to drink out of." She tried to blink away the tears, but they kept filling her eyes and flowing down her cheeks. "She's had our son—known him—longer than we have."

Joe looked out the door, toward the sunlight. He clenched his jaw and tried to pretend that Marcie was someone else, one of the women he saw at the satellite office of NCMEC. But he knew that was a futile effort, for two reasons. First, she was his wife and she was talking about his son. But second, every time he met a mother or a father whose child had been taken from them, he felt the same way. The tarnished armor he tried to keep in place to protect himself from the pain of loss was barely more effective against strangers than it was against his and Marcie's personal anguish. He supposed his empathy for the heartbroken parents made him good at his job, but he was worried that his roiling emotions were going to cripple him in his search for his own child.

As he started to push the screen door open, Marcie shouted, "Joe!"

"What?" he asked distractedly.

"Your phone."

Then he heard it: his phone making a peculiar dinging sound. He froze.

"Is that—?"

He managed to nod. "A message."

"That's the picture," Marcie said breathlessly. "Oh, Joe, I'm afraid to look."

So was he. Reluctantly, he took the phone out of his

pocket and pressed the button to activate the screen. There, on top of a little icon that looked like a mailing envelope, was the number one, indicating that he had one new text message.

With Marcie hanging on to his arm with both hands, he tapped the envelope on the screen with a finger. For a second nothing happened, then a photo appeared.

It was a picture of a little boy, a toddler who could have been two or three years old. His hair was brown and had been dampened and combed back so that the slight widow's peak on his forehead was visible. His blue eyes, so much like his mother's, sparkled in the light from the camera's flash.

Marcie burst into tears and her nails dug into Joe's arm. "It's Joshua. Oh, my baby. My Joshua. Look at him. He's grown so big—" Her voice gave out and her entire body shook with her sobs. "Look at him, Joe. Look at him."

Joe was having trouble believing his eyes. He saw what Marcie saw, and his first reaction was that it was Joshua. But could he be 100 percent sure? Joshua at nine months had had chubby cheeks and a cute up-turned nose that didn't look like either his or Marcie's. This child's nose was straight and had a rounded tip. It still didn't look like his or Marcie's nose, but if he let himself, he could believe the boy's eyes were just like Marcie's. "Marcie, take it easy. We've got to be sure."

"You're not sure?" she exclaimed. "Well, I am. I carried him inside me for nine months. I watched him and held him and fed him and took care of him for another nine months." She jabbed her finger at the phone's screen. "That is my baby!"

At that instant, the phone dinged again and a second message appeared. When the picture came up, it was of the little T-shirt their baby had been wearing when he was stolen. The label said Joshua Joseph Powers. Below the name was his birth date.

Joe's throat closed up. He could barely breathe, much less talk. Marcie had clapped a hand over her mouth and now sobbed loudly. The phone rang, startling Joe as it vibrated. Marcie stood close as he answered, so he held the phone slightly away from his ear so she could hear, too.

"So now do you believe me?" Howard's slimy voice slithered through the receiver.

"Where are you?" Joe demanded. "Is Rhoda with you? Where is my son? Because I know you're not at Rhoda's house."

"Now you listen to me. All you need to know is I've got your kid. And if you want him back it's going to cost you half a million in cash."

Marcie gasped at the man's words.

"Half a million? You're crazy," Joe croaked. "I don't have that kind of money. Not in my wildest dreams. I might be able to scrape together a hundred thousand. Be reasonable. You can do a lot with a hundred thousand dollars."

"Now Mr. Joe Powers, even if you ain't got that money yourself, you and I both know where you can get it easy enough." Howard coughed harshly on his end of the line. "But I'm a reasonable man, Joey. I know it takes time. I'll give you plenty of time—twenty-four hours. When I call you back you'd better be ready to do exactly what I say. And don't forget. If you talk to the police, little Joshy's fingers start coming off and your wife starts getting presents."

The line went dead.

Marcie moaned. As Joe hung up, she stepped away from him. "What did he mean, he knows where you can get the money?"

Joe shrugged and shook his head, still looking at his cell phone.

"Why would he think we could get that kind of money? I wonder what he's talking about?"

"I don't know. We can't worry about that. Come on. I want to get home and look at this photo on the computer screen. I want to study it—see if there's anything in the background that might tell us where he's holding Joshua."

On the drive home, both of them were silent. Joe pulled up to the curb in front of the house and got out. Marcie followed him inside, not even commenting when he unlocked the door with the key he'd never given back to her.

While he headed to the study to transfer the picture to the desktop computer, she went upstairs to wash her face and hands, still carrying the plastic building block. She set it on the edge of the sink while she splashed water on her face. After patting her face dry with a towel, she glanced into the mirror, the towel still pressed against her nose and mouth. Her eyes were red and swollen from crying, but they sparkled with hope. A thrill fluttered through her chest like a butterfly. They'd found Joshua. Her baby. Now all they needed to do was pay the man and bring their little boy home.

She tossed the towel toward the drying rack, picked up the block and walked across the hall to the nursery. She turned on the light. Just like every time she went into Joshua's room, her heart squeezed and her eyes and throat stung with tears. She did her best to not view the room through the eyes of a grieving mother. It was different this time. She had to make everything ready for Joshua's homecoming.

Right now, the room was furnished for an infant. The baby bed would have to be converted to a toddler's bed. The changing table would have to go, as well. She could get a small table and chairs like the one at Rhoda's house, and a blackboard. A poignant smile lit Marcie's face as she imagined Joshua sitting at the table while she taught him letters and words. Her baby had grown into a little boy and she'd missed it, but now they had found him. She set the block on the dresser, turning it so that the *J* faced outward.

Her mood slightly brighter, she headed downstairs. Joe was at the computer, and Joshua's face filled the screen. Marcie gasped in surprise when she saw it. "Oh, Joe. Look at him. What's he holding?"

Joe zoomed in on Joshua's hands, so close Marcie could see the date on the newspaper he held.

"It's today's! It's Joshua and he's okay! Joe!"

Joe clicked the mouse to zoom the photo outward until the full photo was visible.

"He's crying. Do you think they hurt him?" Marcie said, her voice breaking. She reached out as if to wipe the tears off his cheeks. "Zoom in. I want to look at his face."

"I'm trying to see what kind of place they're holding him in. But it's dark."

"Do you think they're making him stay in the dark?"

"No, hon," Joe said. "See? I misspoke. It's not really that dark, just a little too dim to see much of the room. You're positive that's Joshua?"

"What? Of course it is. Why would you ask?"

"It's been two years. I just need to be absolutely sure."

Marcie put her hand on his shoulder and squeezed. "Go back up to his eyes. Remember that tiny mole just above his right eyelid?"

"Tiny mole?"

She chuckled. "It's just above the fold of his right eyelid. See? Right there?"

Joe looked more closely. "That's a mole? I never noticed it."

"You're just his father. I'm his mother," she said teasingly, leaning down and pressing her cheek against his hair.

He sighed deeply in relief. He looked up at her. "It's Joshua."

"Our child is alive. He's healthy. I don't think he's crying there because he's hurt. I think he's angry—probably because he has to hold the paper." She pointed at the screen. "See the little wrinkle in his forehead? He always looks like that when he doesn't get what he wants. Such a deep little frown."

She smiled and went on. "The woman took good care of him, and now we're going to get him back. I'm not sure I've ever been so happy in my life." She took a long breath. "I can't wait to have him back."

"I know," Joe said. "Me, too. I wish I could have gotten a glimpse of him at Rhoda's house, but I did hear her talking to him. She does love him. And he called her Gramma. I think you're absolutely right. I think he's just fine."

Joe switched screens and pulled up the second photo that Howard had sent. It was a close-up of the label inside the neck of the tiny shirt Joshua had been wearing the day he was abducted. Joe studied it, then zoomed in and studied it some more. "It's blurred," he muttered.

Marcie leaned in and looked at it more closely. "Yes, but you can make out the letters, colors and pattern. It's one of the labels your mother had monogrammed for us when he was born."

"You sewed all those in his clothes?"

"Yes," she said. "You mean you never noticed?"

He was still studying the label. "I knew there were labels with his name on them, but I couldn't tell you what they looked like. You're a hundred percent positive?"

"Yes. The font, the color and my awful, uneven stitching. I still have some, if you want to compare."

He shook his head. "Nope." He leaned back in his chair and rubbed his eyes, then got up and started pacing.

"What's wrong?" Marcie asked. "Is it the money?"

"Of course it's the money," he said. "In fact, I need

to go to the bank and get it. I have no idea what I'm going to tell them."

"You don't have to tell them anything, do you? How much do we…do you have anyway? Do you really have a hundred thousand dollars?"

Joe gave her a searching look. "Marcie, *we* have a little over a hundred thousand, plus Joshua's trust that Kit set up, which we can't touch." He frowned. "I guess I could borrow another hundred K from her, with Joshua's trust as collateral."

"Oh," Marcie said as a thought occurred to her. Kit Powers, Joe's mother, was rolling in money. "Maybe that's why they thought you could get half a million dollars. Because you're her son."

Joe didn't answer her. He'd stopped pacing and was staring toward the window with a pained expression on his face.

"Joe? What is it?"

"Hmm?" His gaze met hers. "Oh. Nothing. I was just thinking about Joshua. About how much of his life we've missed." He held out his arms to her and she stepped into the circle of his embrace, sighing as he enveloped her in the warm strength of his arms.

"I know. He's a big boy now. I need to change his room. Convert the baby bed into a toddler bed, get him a table and chairs where we can work on his letters and numbers."

Joe's arms tightened. "Hey, you're not going to cry again are you?"

"It's just that I'm afraid that man will hurt him."

"Hey." Joe pulled away to look down at her. He

touched her cheek. "Rhoda's there. You saw from her house how well she was caring for him. She'll keep him safe."

"Promise me," she said. "Promise me we'll have our baby back here wi—" She stopped before the words *with us* could escape her lips.

Joe bent his head and placed his mouth near her ear, his warm breath playing over her cheek and jaw. "We're going to get him back, Marcie. I swear." He pressed his lips to her ear, then scattered small kisses across the line of her jaw, up her cheek and temple to her forehead and down her nose. He drew in a deep breath and touched the corner of her mouth with his lips.

She parted her lips and sighed and Joe kissed her. It was soft yet firm, not deep or sexual. It was a reassuring kiss, a comforting kiss, and it brought tears to Marcie's eyes.

"Our son is coming home," he whispered, then pulled her close and tightened his embrace.

She hugged him back. "Thank you, Joe," she said softly. "Thank you.

"You look worried," she said, laying her head against his shoulder. "Are you afraid we don't have enough money?"

"Not really," he replied, pressing his cheek against her hair. But then he let go of her and backed away. "But it's going to take a while to get it all together. So I'd better get going."

"What should I do?"

"Stay by the phone, just in case. I'll unforward it

from my phone. I sure don't want to be talking to him while I'm trying to withdraw every dime we have."

"But, Joe, I don't want to talk to him, either. What if I say something wrong?"

"Just follow your instincts. I don't think he'll call back until tomorrow, like he said. But if he does, you just yell and scream at him like I know you want to, okay?" He kissed her forehead. "You'll do fine."

Marcie watched him walk out to the car, then she glanced around her. The kitchen was clean. She'd vacuumed the whole house just a couple of days before. There was nothing else she could think of that needed to be done. On the hall table, just inside the front door, she saw the pile of newspapers that she'd tossed there. That's what she could do. She'd have a cup of coffee and see if she could catch up on the past few days' news. She doubted she could concentrate enough to get through all the newspapers, but she could at least glance through them. She picked them up and headed to the kitchen. Maybe they would keep her occupied until Joe got back.

Chapter Six

"Joshy!" Rhoda said sternly. "I know you're tired of hot dogs, but that's all we've got, other than cereal and an apple." Thanks to that idiot Howard, who had no idea what three-year-olds ate. "Want some cereal?"

"Ceweal!" Joshy said. "Gramma has ceweal!" He toddled over to where his bouncy ball had rolled to a stop and picked it up. He threw it with all his might. It sailed about four feet and bounced against the metal wall and came back toward him. He giggled and tried to catch it.

"Get over here then. I have to hold the bowl, because stupid Howard didn't give us a table. He was probably afraid I'd take one of the legs off and hit him over the head with it." She poured milk from the cooler over the oat rings.

"Oh, no. Tupid Howarr," Joshy said, running over to the cot where Rhoda was sitting. "Me hold it."

"No. I'll hold it. Now be a good boy and eat." She let Joshy pick up the spoon and feed himself while she held the bowl close to him in case he spilled. While she waited for him to finish, she looked around the small wooden building. She knew what this place was. Howard slept here when he spent several nights on Bayou Picou, fishing. She didn't know whom it belonged to, but she'd been there on a couple of rare fishing trips with him. It had dark shutters on the windows, a portable chemical toilet and a gas generator. The lights were on right now, but she knew he couldn't run the generator 24/7, so she wondered what his plans were. If he had any. Knowing him, he hadn't thought past getting her and Joshy away from her house and making sure there was nothing in this place she could use as a weapon or a means of breaking out.

Joshy was finished with his cereal. He leaned down and slurped at the bowl, then peered up at her. "Gramma, look. I'n a good boy."

Rhoda smiled and kissed him on the forehead. "Yes, you are. Are you done now?"

He nodded as milk rolled down his chin.

A loud banging echoed through the building. Joshy jumped and started crying. "It's okay, darling," Rhoda said. "It's just stupid Howard."

Rhoda set Joshy's bowl on the counter while she listened to Howard undo the padlock that kept the cabin locked. Joshy clung to her side.

"Rhoda!" Howard called. "Get away from the door. I ain't about to have you trying to attack me and getting out the door." The door swung slowly open, revealing Howard standing on the balls of his feet, apparently ready to rush her if she tried anything.

Rhoda laughed at him. "You're such an idiot, Howard. I'm not going to try anything that might put Joshy in danger. You'll screw up soon enough and Joshy and I will just walk right out of here."

"Rho, I need help," Howard said. "I've gotta figure out a foolproof way to get the money and get us out of here without getting caught and hopefully without getting anybody hurt."

"Right," she said. "Good luck with that. I hope you brought us some water. I couldn't find any. And what are you going to do about that generator? I know you can't leave it on all the time, but we're going to need light, and if there comes a late cool spell we'll need heat."

"Aw, woman, quit your bitching. I'm going to take care of everything. I'll turn the generator off at night when you two are tucked in, and I'll turn it on in the morning, about the time you get up. We're supposed to have a thermostat and timer for it, but there's a couple of folks who haven't ponied up the money yet."

"We're going to need more blankets then. Howard, why'd you have to bring us out here? What do you think I'm gonna do? Call the police? It wouldn't take them ten minutes to figure out who he is," she whispered.

"No, I don't think you'll call the police. I think you'll take that kid and run. And I don't want that, Rho." He sat down on the cot. "I told 'em half a mil, Rho. Half a million dollars. I told Powers if he didn't have that kind of money he knew where he could get it. I was talking about the Delanceys," he finished with a sheepish grin.

"And now you need me to plan how you're going to get the money? Well, forget it. I've never been so mad at anyone in my life than I am at you right now. And

I promise you first chance I get, I'm going to *K-I-L-L* you. Now get up. Joshy needs to go to sleep."

Howard stood with a grunt.

"Come on, Joshy," she called. "Let's get in the bed. Time for you to go to sleep."

"But, Gramma, it's light out. Play ball?" Joshy said, peering around Rhoda's back at Howard. "Howarr, you go."

Howard laughed. "Hey, Rho, the kid's a smart-a—"

"Don't talk like that around him," Rhoda interrupted. "If you want any help from me, you'd better get us better accommodations."

"Good grief, woman, what else could you ask for? There's electricity, food, bottled water to drink—"

"I need water to clean with," she insisted.

"I got you a five-gallon jug of water. It's sitting right outside the door. You can come and get it."

"What? You get it."

"Aw, hell, no. You're liable to run out. Heck no."

"Me and Joshy are going to get into bed and read picture books, since there's nothing else to do here. We'll sit on the cot while you bring the water in. Then you can go start making arrangements for a better place for us to stay."

"You've already got food and water. I got toys for the kid and books for you. What else do you want? A big-screen TV?"

Rhoda scowled at him. "It doesn't have to be big-screen. And how about a microwave, and some more fruit. Yogurt, a couple of those microwavable complete meals that don't have to be refrigerated. *Coffee* would be nice."

Howard gaped at her. "Anything else, your highness? If I get you some of that, you'll help me?"

"If you get me *some* of that, I won't be waiting for you with an iron bar from that cot across your thick skull next time you come here. If you get me *all* of it, I might decide to help you, depending on what your plans are on the off chance this stupid scheme works."

From behind her, on the cot, Joshy murmured, "Tupid Howarr."

MARCIE PACED FROM the foyer to the kitchen and back, over and over again. Every time she walked into the kitchen, her eyes went straight to the section of newspaper that she'd folded and laid on the counter and her anger ramped up another few notches.

She picked up the paper, skimmed the article again, although by now she could quote it word for word, then slapped it back down on the table.

When she'd first spotted Joe's photo splashed across a double column, she'd stared in disbelief and shock. Then she'd read the headline—Local Attorney's Connection with Delanceys Shocks New Orleans—and skimmed the short piece.

Joe? Her Joe was the illegitimate son of Con Delancey? For a moment, the words floated around in her brain like letters in alphabet soup and all she could do was wait for them to settle down. She felt the numb tingling of shock all the way to her fingertips, although why, she wasn't sure. His mother was Kit Powers, Con

Delancey's long-time mistress. It made perfect sense that they'd had a child together.

Other things made sense now, too, like what Howard had said to Joe about getting the money. *If you ain't got that money yourself, you and I both know where you can get it easy enough.* Joe's kidnapped son was a Delancey. Joe could go to the Delanceys for the money.

Or could he? Everyone knew how the Delanceys felt about family. But they, like everyone else in the New Orleans metropolitan area, had seen the paper by now. How were they reacting to the news that Con Delancey had a bastard son?

She found herself back in the foyer, looking through the sidelights at the street, dimly lit with street lamps. Where was he? She looked at her watch. Anger bloomed in her chest, squeezing the air from her lungs. He'd known all this and hadn't told her. But when? When had he known? Just yesterday? Had he read the article with as much shock and trepidation as she had? Or had his mother told him years ago? It didn't matter. In either case, he'd kept it from her.

But why? Embarrassment? Shame? Some misguided notion of protecting her or Joshua? Whatever the reason and no matter how angry she was, her heart ached for him. Through all the years they'd been together, he'd never talked about his dad. Whenever she'd tried to bring it up, he'd changed the subject or shut down. She'd always figured, given his mother's lifestyle, that he didn't know who his father was. That maybe even Kit didn't know. Marcie had always resented Kit for that reason.

But whether Joe had known for hours or years, he should have told her. She was his wife. They had a child together. If anyone in the world deserved to know the truth about his parentage, it was her.

She thought about what he'd said as he'd left earlier. What if he had gone to the Delanceys to ask for the money without even consulting her?

She stalked back into the kitchen, picked up the paper and ripped the article out of it. She heard Joe's car pull into the driveway. She clenched her fist, crushing the newsprint.

JOE UNLOCKED THE front door and stepped inside. "Marcie?" He looked down the hall toward the kitchen, but didn't see her. He glanced into the living room and past it into the dining room as he walked across the tile foyer and into the kitchen. Marcie was standing at the French doors, looking out into the darkness.

"Where have you been?" she asked without turning around.

"I told you, to try and put together the money Howard is demanding. I also went by the office to see if I could find a Howard that lives in Killian or the surrounding area."

"It's late."

"Not really," he said. "It's just a little after seven."

She didn't comment on the time. "So how much money did you manage to get?"

He looked at her rigid back and slightly lifted head. "Marcie? What's wrong? Has something happened?

Did Howard call back?" He started toward her, but she whirled to face him and held up a hand.

"Don't," she said. She held out her other hand, which held a wrinkled, torn piece of a newspaper.

The paper was crushed almost into a wad, but that didn't matter. He recognized it. It was the article. She'd found it. His stomach felt like it had sunk to his knees.

"Did you drive over to Chef Voleur?"

"What?" he asked automatically, still staring at the article. "Chef Voleur? Why—? Oh. No, Marcie, I—" He stopped at the look in her eyes. If they were lasers his head would be exploding right now.

"Really? You didn't go to the Delanceys and ask them for five hundred thousand dollars to pay a kidnapper for their grandson?"

"No, I didn't. I have no reason to go to the Delanceys for money."

Her glare didn't cool one degree. "No? Do you think I can't read, Joe? That I wouldn't see this? That I can't figure out what's happening here? This—" she waved the wrinkled piece of newsprint "—is why our son has been kidnapped. That man read this article and figured he could get money from the Delanceys."

Joe closed his eyes and shook his head. "I only found out a few days ago."

"Really?" she said acidly. "You're almost thirty years old and your mother never told you who your father was?"

"That's right," he said. "She came to see me on her way to her yoga class the other day. She told me that a police detective, Ethan Delancey, had come to see her.

Said he had something she needed to see. And she, in turn, thought I needed to see it. Big of her, right? After all this time? I never asked about my father. I figured she didn't know." He shrugged. "I…never cared."

Marcie stared at him. "Well, maybe you care now. Because it's obvious that the reason these people have suddenly decided to demand a ransom for the child they *stole* and kept for two years as their own, is because they now know he's a Delancey."

Joe nodded. He didn't have an answer for her.

"So why didn't you go to them for the money?"

Her question shocked him. "Why—? Marcie, why do you *think* I didn't go to them? This is not their problem. They have no reason to give me anything. The Delanceys never knew Joshua existed. Hell, they didn't know *I* existed."

Marcie's cheeks flushed with anger and she held up the article again. "They know now, don't you think?"

He nodded, not looking at her. He knew she had a right to be angry. But he wished she'd get over it and help him figure out what to do. He was angry, too, and frightened for their son. "You aren't seriously suggesting I go walking up to their door and say, 'Hi, I'm Joe Powers, your long-lost brother/uncle/whatever, and I need half a million in cash, thank you very much.'"

Marcie's face began to crumple. "That's exactly what you should do. My baby is out there, possibly cold and scared. I don't even know if anyone is with him. They're holding him hostage somewhere. He could be all alone. And if the only way I can ever see my son again is by crawling to the Delanceys and begging them for help, then I will do that."

"No, you won't!" Joe thundered. "They are *not* my family! I may happen to have been born because one of Con Delancey's feisty little swimmers made it upstream to my mother's—" He stopped. "I'm not a Delancey and I'm not going to go to them begging for money. I'll take care of my son myself."

Marcie folded her arms across her middle, a sure sign that she knew she was losing the argument. "They would give it to you," she said stubbornly.

"Do you have any concept of how many people contact a family like the Delanceys every year, claiming they're a long-lost relative? They'd have been broke long ago."

"But you really are," she said, still hugging herself, her eyes sunken and sad.

Joe started to speak, stopped, then started again. "It's not going to happen." His voice was flat and hard. He hated to talk to her like that, but she was headed down a dangerous path.

"How—how much money were you able to get?"

Joe looked down at his feet. "I took out all our savings and cashed out every asset I could convert to cash. Then I went to Kit."

Marcie moaned. Joe knew why. She didn't like the idea of being in debt to Joe's mother. She thought of Kit as a cold, calculating businesswoman who neglected and endangered her son by the lifestyle she led.

"Joe? How much?"

He put his hands in his pants pockets. "I managed to get a hundred and seventy thousand."

"Now? You have it now?"

He nodded.

"Surely that will be enough. Maybe we convince him that if we go to the Delanceys the media and everybody will know something's up. That photographers and reporters are all following you looking for a story. If he holds out for half a million, he might end up with nothing, or in prison."

"Yeah. That makes sense, but I'm not sure Howard would agree."

"What else can we do? Can we borrow against the house or take a second mortgage?"

"That might yield us another hundred thousand, but it wouldn't be enough. Not if he insists on half a million."

"This is such a nightmare. I thought these past two years—not knowing if Joshua was alive—were the worst thing I'd ever had to live with. But now, knowing his life is in the hands of a man who only cares about money?" Marcie pressed her knuckles to her lips. "I'm terrified I'm never going to see my baby again."

Chapter Seven

Neither Joe nor Marcie were very hungry, so Joe fixed an omelet that they picked over, then by ten-thirty they were both in bed, Marcie in the master bedroom and Joe in the nursery on the sofa bed.

It was still dark when he turned over and opened his eyes, disturbed by a sound. His first sleepy instinct was that it was Joshua crying, but immediately, he realized his mistake. Joshua wasn't here. He picked up his phone and hit a button, checking the time. It wasn't even midnight.

The sound came again. This time he recognized it. It was Marcie, crying, like she'd done so many nights after Joshua's disappearance. He could hear her clearly, because he'd left the nursery door open, hoping it would help the air to circulate and dissipate the scent of baby powder that made him dream of his son.

He lay there for a couple of minutes, listening to her heartbreaking, muffled sobs, thinking maybe she was asleep and just dreaming about Joshua, and any moment now she'd wake up or turn over. But the sobs went on and on.

He got up and tiptoed over to her door, which was ajar, just like it had been for the nine months after Joshua had been born. They'd had baby monitors and even a baby cam, but she'd still insisted that the door be left open, in case the power went out or something else untoward happened.

Standing at the open door, Joe saw the outline of her body in the faint light from the window. She seemed so small in the king-sized bed. But the curve of her hip stirred memories of nights filled with lovemaking and laughter and a deep, sweet love that he realized would last forever, even if *they* did not.

Her body shook slightly as she cried, her shoulders hunched and her face buried in a pillow.

"Marcie?" he whispered.

The sobbing stopped suddenly.

"Hon, are you okay?"

Her breath caught, then she sniffled. After a few seconds, she said, "I'm…f-fine."

"Right," he countered gently. "You sound fine. Want some water or something?"

"No."

"Something else to drink?"

"No."

He pushed the door open farther and stepped inside. "Want to talk?" he asked, doubting seriously that she'd take him up on that offer.

She didn't speak right away. He heard more sniffles, then she cleared her throat. "Maybe," she whispered, surprising him. "Do you want to…sit…on the bed?"

He sat down on top of the covers. He had on boxer

shorts and a T-shirt, as much or more than he'd ever worn in bed with her, so he didn't feel uncomfortable. Not totally anyhow. His eyes were dilated, so he could see her dim outline as she sat up and pushed a pillow behind her back. He reached out and caught her hand.

"Tell me what's wrong," he said.

"What's wrong?" she began harshly, then stopped herself. She pulled in a deep breath and let it out slowly. "It's just everything, Joe. Finding Joshua, losing him again. You. The money—you know. How impossible it's going to be to get enough to satisfy that man."

He heard the desperation in her voice and recognized it. Squeezing her hand in an attempt at comfort, he nodded, as much to himself as to her. He'd felt overwhelmed and desperate every second of the past two years.

"Did you find Howard?" she asked.

"What?"

"Howard. You said earlier that you'd looked up all the Howards in Killian? Did you find him? I mean, how many could there be? Hopefully only a few."

"Yeah, there were four," he said. "One is in his eighties. One in his twenties, and two who could be our Howard's age. Of those two, one is a teacher at the grade school. There was almost no information about the last one, Howard Lelievre."

"Le-leave?" Marcie said, trying out the name. "That's the man who has Joshua?"

"Lelievre. It's a Cajun name and it's sure not spelled like it sounds." He spelled it for her.

"Do you think we can call the police now? Now that we know who he is? Oh, my God, we can't," she said, answering her own question before Joe could. "He said he'd hurt Joshua."

"I'm sorry, hon," Joe said. "I wish there were a way to bring the police in to help us."

Marcie clutched at his arm. "We've got to do something, Joe. What about some kind of an anonymous message? You know like, 'I have information that Howard Lelievre, of Killian, Louisiana, may be holding a child that belongs to someone else.'"

"What are the police going to do with that? With no names and no proof that he has the child, it's hardly probable cause."

"Probable—? Could you stop with all the legal mumbo jumbo? I am so sick of hearing it. If the police got a message like that about a child, aren't they required to investigate? Maybe the message could say 'child that belongs to Joe and Marcie Powers.' What about that, Joe? Would that be probable cause?" Her voice had gotten shrill.

"Even if they didn't decide it was a hoax spurred by the newspaper article, I'm not sure they could do anything more than drive out to Rhoda's house and ask a few questions of neighbors." He sighed. "No. We've got to do this ourselves, and we're going to have to think like Howard thinks. What if the police do go out there looking for him? What do you think he'll do? What will he think?"

She was silent.

"I mean it, Marcie. You know the answer to that. What's Howard going to think?"

After a moment, she said sheepishly, "He's going to

think that we called the police. But if he calls us, we could tell him we didn't." She held up her hands. "I know. I know. Why would he believe us? But, Joe, we've got to do something. I'll die if that man hurts Joshua."

Her voice was even and soft, but he heard and recognized the desperation behind her words. The feeling seethed inside him, too. "I know, hon. I think I might die, too, if we can't get him back safe and sound."

Marcie turned toward him and he held out his arm, just as he had so many nights as they settled in to sleep. It was a little awkward since she was under the covers and he was on top of them. Still, she sank into his side, resting her head on the curve of his shoulder. "I'm sorry, Joe."

"Sorry?" he said. "What for?"

"I don't mean to take everything out on you. You've always taken care of everything. I guess I'm used to you being able to fix any problem."

"If there were anything I could do—"

"I know," she said, putting her hand on his chest and spreading her fingers. "I know you would."

He tightened his arm around her shoulders and pulled her closer. Her head lay in the hollow between his shoulder and arm. It fit there perfectly. He pressed his face into her sweetly scented hair.

"Joe?"

"Hmm," he responded quietly.

"Could you sleep in here tonight? I think I'll sleep better with you here."

"Sure," he said. "I'll lie down in the recliner."

"No. Please, stay here." She patted the covers be-

side her. "I'll feel better with you here. Safe. Even...
hopeful."

Joe sighed. He wanted to warn her not to be too hopeful. It was an endlessly torturous feeling, he knew. It
meant waking up suddenly in the middle of the night,
with a new idea about how to go about searching for
their son. It meant not being able to concentrate on work
or anything else, because his mind was occupied with
trying to remember one more detail about those critical few seconds while he was taking his credit card out
of his wallet instead of watching his son. But he didn't
want to destroy the only frayed thread holding Marcie
together. That last fragile ray of hope. He knew exactly
how fragile it was because it was all that held him together, too.

After slipping under the covers, Joe pulled a pillow
under his head. "Try to get some sleep, hon. We need
to be rested, in case something happens."

"Like what?" she asked, stiffening beside him.
"What do you think is going to happen?"

He leaned over and kissed her on the top of her head,
then turned his back to her. "All I'm saying is, that while
we can, we need to rest. So close your eyes, sleepy-
head."

For a few moments, all was silent. Joe was drifting
off when he felt Marcie's hand on his back. She ran her
fingers up his spine to the nape of his neck, then he felt
her lift her head and kiss him there.

"Marcie?" he said, half convinced he was dreaming.
When she answered, "Hmm?" in his ear, he realized

that she was actually kissing his neck and the curve of his shoulder.

"What are you doing?" he asked.

"Saying good-night," she murmured. "This feels good." Kiss. "Right." Kiss. "Familiar." She planted the third kiss on the center of his back between his shoulder blades.

He turned onto his back and Marcie slipped beneath his arm, but she didn't lay her head on his shoulder. Instead she bent and kissed him on the side of the head, near his ear.

For some reason, her advances scared him. "Marcie?" he said, taking hold of her shoulders and studying her. "Are you all right?"

"Of course I am. Why? Do you think I'm asleep?" She smiled at him. "I can guarantee I'm not."

"Then what is this?"

"I thought you'd be happy to make love with me—" She paused. "I'm...sorry."

"Hey," he said, tightening his arm around her. "I have always been happy to make love to you. I just don't want you thinking you have to, or—"

Marcie bent her head and kissed him on the mouth. When she was done, she looked down at him. "Did that feel like I *had* to?" she asked, a small smile playing around her mouth. "I want to feel good, Joe. I want to hold you and be held by you. I want what we used to have."

Joe pulled Marcie to him and turned them both so that he was above her, then he pressed kisses along her cheek and jaw and down the column of her neck. Then he kissed her mouth, delving deeply, kissing her like a lover, like the lovers they'd been and still were. He moaned deep in his throat when she pressed herself more tightly against him and wrapped her arms around him. Desire grew into arousal and blossomed between them as it always had, quickening their pulses and driving sad thoughts out of their heads.

Marcie wanted Joe with a poignant, quiet desire that had built inside of her during the months they'd been apart. She had missed him so much. When he sank into her, he filled her the way she had longed for him to. It was like becoming whole. She exhaled in an exquisite sigh of desire, then soared quickly to a climax that seemed to go on forever. Finally drained, she collapsed against the bedclothes.

Joe groaned and found his own release in one last long thrust. Then he lay carefully atop Marcie, his weight suspended on his elbows and knees. "Hey," he whispered. "You okay?"

To his relief, she nodded. "I'm good, Joe. Really good." She yawned and stretched and he took the opportunity to kiss the soft underside of her chin.

"Yes, you are," he said. "In fact, I might go so far as to say you're spectacular."

Then he heard a beautiful, welcome sound, one he hadn't heard in a long time: Marcie chuckling.

THE NEXT MORNING when Joe came downstairs, he heard Marcie in the kitchen and smelled the delicious scent of freshly made coffee. He figured she'd be pacing back and forth with her mug, sipping nervously, wondering when Howard was going to call. He knew exactly how she felt. He wasn't prone to pacing, like she was, but he had woken up as nervous as a cat, wondering just exactly when the phone call would come, and what demands Howard would make.

As he descended the last stair he saw a car pull up to the curb through the sidelight of the front door. He watched as a tall, lean man in a sport coat and slacks got out of the car and walked up to ring the doorbell. He didn't recognize the man, but there seemed to be something familiar about him. Joe was pretty sure who he was, and if he were right, this morning house call was not going to be pleasant.

He opened the door before the doorbell rang.

"Hi," the man said, holding out a badge in a leather case. "I'm NOPD Detective Ethan Delancey. You're Joseph Powers?"

"That's right," Joe said. He kept his voice even, but he couldn't help glancing past the detective, wondering if Howard were smart enough or organized enough to have someone watching the house.

Delancey's eyes narrowed and Joe knew the detective had seen him checking the street for other cars.

"I wonder if I could come in for a minute," he said. "I'd like to ask you a couple of questions."

"About what?" Joe asked, carefully keeping his voice and his expression neutral. He didn't know what Delancey wanted, but none of the possibilities he could think of were palatable to him. And none of them boded good news.

The detective showed his first glint of emotion. For

a split second, Joe saw a hint of vague discomfort pass across his expression. "I spoke with your mother the other day."

"I'm aware of that," Joe said, still politely neutral.

"Mr. Powers, I can assure you, this won't take long."

Joe sighed. It was obvious that if he didn't let Detective Delancey in, the two of them could stand there all day, being eternally polite and quietly obstinate. He stepped back just far enough to allow the detective to ease past him into the foyer.

As they crossed into the living room, Marcie came through the dining room door. "Hello," she said to the visitor as she wiped her hands on a dish towel. She glanced nervously at Joe.

"Marcie, this is Detective Delancey." Before Joe could go any further, Delancey spoke up.

"Mrs. Powers," he said, nodding. "I just have a matter to discuss with your husband. It shouldn't take long." His voice was polite but dismissive.

A frown wrinkled Marcie's brow as she looked at the detective, then at Joe. She paused, as if making up her mind about something. "Would you like some coffee?" she said sweetly.

"No, ma'am. I've had too much today already."

"Joe? Coffee?"

"I'll wait," Joe said. "We should be done here in a few minutes."

Marcie's frown deepened. "Don't forget—"

He waved a hand. "Don't worry. But if necessary, you go ahead and handle it."

She opened her mouth, then closed it again. After a

second, she nodded. "I'll be upstairs then." She turned on her heel and left. He heard her footsteps on the stairs.

Joe turned to Delancey and gestured vaguely toward the sofa.

Delancey propped on the edge of the cushion, his elbows on his knees. "I won't take up much of your time, Mr. Powers, but I wanted to follow up with you on the matter I mentioned to your mother."

"Yes?" Joe didn't plan to give the detective anything. He wondered if Delancey had been dispatched by the family to issue the official Delancey welcome to the bastard son. If that's what he was doing here, Joe wanted no part of it. He didn't care if the gesture was genuine or for show.

"I assume she told you what I told her."

When Joe didn't react to the question, Delancey went on. "My partner came upon the copy of your birth certificate while doing a warrant search of Senator Darby Sills's personal financial records in his home, office and safety deposit box. I have no idea why Sills had the copy. You've probably seen in the news that he had been blackmailing a couple of people for several years. My best guess is that he'd either tried or planned to try to blackmail my—Con Delancey, regarding your birth."

Joe nodded. That was what he'd figured, too. He glanced at his watch, then sent a quick glance toward the stairs. It was almost nine o'clock. Howard was going to call soon, and he didn't want Delancey here when that phone call came in. "I'm aware of everything you told my mother, Detective. Was there some specific reason you wanted to speak with me about it?"

"May I ask when you first knew that Con Delancey was your father?"

"I suppose you may," Joe countered as he decided it was time for the detective to leave. He stood. "I found out that your grandfather was my father when my mother came to see me at my office after she talked to you."

Delancey stood, too. "You hadn't known before that?"

Joe shook his head. "If you'll excuse me, Detective, my wife and I are expecting an important phone call, so—"

Ethan Delancey gave Joe a hard look, then walked around him through the foyer and opened the front door. "Mr. Powers, I know about your child, as well. I'm really sorry about your loss."

Grimacing, Joe spoke through gritted teeth. "Thank you," he said, taking hold of the inside knob of the front door, thereby feeling as though he were taking control of the situation. But something in the other man's manner made him feel as though he weren't as in control as he'd like to be.

"You've spent a good deal of time searching in police databases within the past few days, as well as having others searching on your behalf."

"How—?" Joe bit his tongue.

"How do I know?" Delancey replied. "Because I've spent some time searching for you."

"Searching for me?"

"That's right." The detective shrugged. "Call it curiosity. When I first saw your birth certificate, I pretended it didn't bother me that my grandfather had fathered a son that was almost the same age as me. Our birthdays are about a month apart. But I finally had to admit I wanted to know more about you. So I looked up information about you in our database. That's where I read about your child's abduction. Then I found that you actually have access to our database."

"Through my job," Joe said.

Delancey nodded. "So I had one of our computer techs trace what you've looked at, and found out that within the past few days you'd accessed records of four people with the first name Howard in and around Killian. You almost immediately zeroed in on Howard Lelievre. I backtracked from his records and found that his disability check goes to Rhoda Sumner. Turns out that her records were flagged, because a dispatcher in Baton Rouge had run a license plate that turned out to be hers."

Joe looked at his watch. "That's fascinating, Detective, but could you get to the point? Are you here to arrest me for unauthorized use of protected information? I'm an attorney and as I told you, I'm authorized through the NCMEC to access those types of records."

"Not planning to arrest you," Detective Delancey said. "I think I know why you've been looking up everything you can find on Howard and Rhoda. A little digging told me that she has a child that appears to be around two years old."

Joe felt his face drain of color, but he did his best to maintain a neutral expression.

"You think Rhoda's child is your son, don't you?"

There it was. The thing Joe had dreaded since Marcie had given him Rhoda's license plate number. He should have predicted that the person who caught him poking around in the police database for information would be a Delancey. He wiped his face wearily. "I don't think. I know."

"That's what the phone call is, isn't it? It's Howard and Rhoda. They want money."

Joe didn't answer. He studied Ethan for a long time. It wasn't hard to convince himself that there was a resemblance between the two of them. Did his connection with the Delanceys go more than skin-deep? He paced back and forth for a moment, as Ethan stood quietly, watching him.

Finally he decided he had no choice but to confirm what the man already knew. He didn't have a clue what Delancey would do with the information, but it would be difficult for him to make the situation any worse.

"He's going to call this morning. Probably in a few minutes. But, Detective, he'll hurt my son if he knows we've gone to the police. He told Marcie he'd cut off one of Joshua's fingers and send it to her. I can't take that chance. I can't involve the police in any way." He stopped. "I don't know if you can possibly understand—"

Delancey nodded. "Let me explain something quickly. My brother Travis came back to New Orleans recently and found out in a single day that he had a son and that his son had been abducted. My brothers and cousins worked together with Travis to bring his son home safely." He gave Joe a small smile. "You have some things to learn about the Delanceys. We're a very large and very close family. There's nothing I wouldn't do for a brother or a cousin or…an uncle."

The way he said *uncle* hit Joe square in the solar plexus. For the first time, it occurred to him that in terms of genealogy, he *was* Ethan's uncle. An odd sensation fluttered in his chest, but he didn't have the time or the inclination to examine it. Right now his focus was on his son. "What are you saying?" Joe asked.

"I'm saying, you're not involving the police. You're involving your family."

Joe stared at the detective. "You're a police detective. How can you act on your own, outside the protection of your badge and authority?"

The detective shrugged. "It's worked before. You tell me what you need and—"

At that instant Marcie stalked into the room. Joe hadn't heard her footsteps on the stairs. "What's going on here?" she demanded in a shrill voice. "You." She turned to Delancey. "You get out of my house. I don't know why you came, but unless you're placing us under arrest, you have no right to be here."

"That's right, Mrs. Powers," Delancey said. "I don't have a right to be here. My reason for coming was to introduce myself to your husband, who, as it turns out, is my uncle." He gave her an innocent smile.

"Marcie—" Joe began, seeing the growing anger in her expression.

"No," she said, waving a hand at Joe without taking her eyes off Delancey. "Please leave my house, right now."

Joe gritted his teeth. Marcie was right, of course. They couldn't take even the slightest chance that Howard would find out that the detective had been here.

"Certainly, Mrs. Powers," Delancey said, then turned to Joe. "May we exchange phone numbers? Just to be safe?"

They agreed, then Joe walked him to the door.

As he stepped over the threshold, Delancey spoke one more time. "Please call me if you need anything. Our family will help in any way we can."

Chapter Eight

Joe watched until the detective got into his car and drove away. Then he walked into the kitchen where Marcie was just pouring him a cup of coffee. She set the cup on the counter and folded her arms.

Joe picked it up and muttered, "Thanks," as he blew on it.

"That man's name was Delancey?"

Joe nodded. "Detective Ethan Delancey."

"What was he doing here?"

"He's the one who told Kit they'd found my birth certificate."

Marcie stared at him. "So did he come here to tell you about it?"

"No. He assumed I already knew."

"Well, then, why was he here? And why was he talking about doing anything he could to help us. Joe, you told me you didn't go to the Delanceys. If you didn't, then what was that detective doing here and how did he know we need help?"

"Hon, I'm not lying to you. He's been looking up information about me. Curiosity about the bastard son,

I guess. So he saw in the police database where I ran Rhoda's license plate and searched for Howard. He figured out what was going on."

"He figured it out on his own?" she said doubtfully. "Joe, he's going to ruin everything. If Howard finds out that the police are—" A sob tore from her throat and she pressed her knuckles against her teeth. "Oh, my God, he'll hurt my baby. I can't stand it."

Joe reached for her but she backed away. "Marcie, stop it. Stop acting like I'm the enemy here. Now come on, hon. Calm down." He held out his arms. "Come on."

But she stood her ground. After a few seconds, though, she got her breathing under control. She looked up at him with accusing eyes. "What's going to happen now? Are the police going to take over? What's going to happen to Joshua?"

"Listen to me," Joe said, approaching her slowly. He brushed a finger across her cheek where a tear was falling. "Be still and let me tell you what he told me, okay?"

Just as he saw her relax a little and opened his mouth to explain how Detective Ethan Delancey had figured out what was going on, the phone rang.

Joe glanced at Marcie, brows raised, but she shook her head violently. She didn't want to talk to Howard. So he picked up the portable handset. "Hello?"

"Hey, Joe, whaddaya know? How'd you sleep last night?"

Howard's harsh voice grated across his nerves like fingernails on a blackboard. If the man were in the same room, Joe would gladly punch him right in his big, ugly nose.

Marcie stepped up close, so he held the handset so she could hear. The sweet scent of her hair tickled his nose as she leaned in to listen. Turning his head slightly away, he concentrated on dealing with Howard.

"I slept fine, Mr. Lelievre," he said coolly. "How about you? Did you sleep well knowing you're endangering the life of a child and breaking federal law?" He took a deep, fortifying breath and continued before Howard had a chance to speak. "Now you listen to me. I want to talk to my son. I want to ask him who he's with and what his name is and if he's hurt or sad."

Beside him, Marcie made a small, distressed sound.

He went on. "I need proof of life *and* proof that he's not being mistreated before I say another word to you."

"Oh, no, Joe, ol' buddy. You don't call the shots. I do."

"Not this one. If you don't put Joshua on the phone right now, I will hang up and you will get nothing, because I'll know that you don't really have my son."

Marcie's fingernails dug into the flesh of his forearm. He'd told Marcie before that they had to maintain control of the conversation. He knew that was what the FBI taught in their training on dealing with hostage situations. He hoped he was right in this case. He knew that Rhoda was a wild card. Everything he'd seen told him that she had stolen Joshua because she wanted a baby. He doubted that she had agreed to this plan to get money—unless Howard had promised her that they would never turn over the child. That they'd take the money and run.

He held his breath as he waited for Howard to answer.

"You hang up and you'll never see your kid. Now how much money have you got? I hope it's enough."

"Proof of life, Howard. Right now or I'm hanging up. Five. Four. Three—"

"Hey, woman," Howard yelled away from the phone. "Bring the kid over here. Now!"

Joe's pulse sped up. He heard voices in the background.

"Oh, just shut up and do it," Howard groused.

Then Joe heard Rhoda. "Joshy? Come out here, honey."

Joshy. His son. His pulse kicked up so high that he thought he might faint from lack of oxygen. He could barely breathe. Beside him, Marcie's nails dug deeper. Her breaths were short and sharp.

Rhoda said something unintelligible, then Joe heard a small, sweet voice. "Hello? Who's 'is?"

Marcie's breath whooshed out in a combination of sob and sigh. A tightness that hurt like hell squeezed Joe's chest. It felt like the broken shards of his heart were rubbing together, trying to find a fit. *Please,* he prayed. *Please be Joshua.*

"Hi," he said, and his voice cracked. "What's your name?"

"I'n Joshy. I'n a big boy."

Marcie sobbed.

Joe had to swallow the lump in his throat before he could speak. "I'll bet you are. Who's there with you?"

"Gramma and—oh-no Howarr," the toddler said.

It sounded as if Joshy thought that oh-no Howarr was his name. Joe almost laughed. Oh-no Howarr was a good name for the bully. "So, Joshy, do you know where you are right now?"

"Gramma said it's his fishy place."

"Whose fishy place, Joshy?"

"Oh-no Howarr."

"Is the fishy place fun? What are you doing there?"

"No," the child said. "I wan' go home. Dere's no TV here and I hafta eat ceweal. I's oh-no Howarr's fault."

"Gimme that phone, kid!" Howard yelled. "That's enough."

Joshy squealed and Joe heard small footsteps on an echoing hardwood floor. "Gramma! Howarr mean!"

"No!" Marcie cried. "Wait! Joshua, please?"

Marcie's terrified voice shattered Joe's already broken heart. He held his finger to his lips and shook his head.

"Awright, Joe, that's it. You've got your proof. Now—what about the money?"

"Where do you want it?" Joe asked harshly. "Tell me where and when and I'll be there."

"Not hardly," Howard said.

Joe's lungs seized. He grimaced, willing the man not to say the words he knew were coming.

"You don't bring the money. Your pretty wife does. And she comes alone."

"No!" Joe thundered. Marcie tugged on his arm. He didn't want to look at her, didn't want to give her a chance to agree with a dangerous scheme that he wasn't about to allow.

"Yes!" she cried, trying to grab the phone from Joe. "I'll do it. Name the time and place. When? Just tell me and I'll be there."

Howard laughed and the phone went dead.

The sudden dial tone shocked them both into frozen silence. Marcie was leaning on Joe, one hand on his arm and the other around his wrist, as if she could wrestle the phone from him. She let go as if his skin were on fire.

Joe set the phone down and Marcie grabbed it. She hit the code to redial the last number, but nothing happened. She cried out in frustration and slammed the phone down on the table.

"You made him angry!" she accused Joe. "You made him angry and he hung up. What are we going to do now?" She swiped at the tears on her cheeks as if she were swatting flies. But they kept falling. "Oh, dear God, we don't know anything. Why did he hang up?"

Joe picked up the handset and put it back on its cradle. "He thinks he's taken back the upper hand."

"He has," she retorted.

Joe didn't say anything. He picked up his mug, rinsed it, then ran cold water into it and took a long drink.

"Hasn't he?"

"No," he said, turning around. "Look at him. What's he dealing with? A kid that needs feeding, entertaining, maybe medication if he has a cold or an ear infection. And that's all."

Marcie glared at Joe in irritation. How could he be so rational? So smart? He was right, of course. Howard was sitting there with a toddler and no money. "He's going to have to call back," she said.

"Got it in one," Joe responded with a small smile.

No, she thought. You got it in one. You had to feed it to me. "But," she said as a thought occurred to her, "what's going to stop him from ignoring us and calling the Delanceys?" She gasped. "What if he's called them already? What if that's why that detective was here? To see if we'd heard from him? Howard could be playing us both."

"No. Ethan Delancey would have told me if they'd gotten a call. No, if Howard's not a complete idiot, he won't call the Delanceys as long as he thinks we might have gotten money from them. Besides, I never told him how much money I had. I just said we'd bring it to him."

"You've got it all figured out," Marcie said in awe, which earned her a suspicious glance until he apparently decided she wasn't being sarcastic.

"Not really," he said. "I'm playing the odds. If Howard is dumber or, God forbid, a lot smarter than he seems, I could be wrong. But based on the training I got on how to work with abductors, even though he's the one who hung up on us, he'll call back, because he hasn't gotten what he wants yet."

Marcie felt as though she were teetering on the edge of a cliff. She took a shaky breath and wiped her face with both hands, then shoved her fingers into her hair, pushing it back away from her face. "I don't know if I can just sit here until he does call back."

"We can forward the phone to my cell again and

go somewhere. You want to get some breakfast?" He glanced at his watch. "Or lunch?"

She shook her head. "I don't think I can eat," she said. "I'm going to switch from coffee to iced tea. Can I fix you a grilled cheese sandwich or some eggs?"

He sent her a look that she couldn't decipher. "You know I love your grilled cheese," he said. "Thanks."

Such a polite answer to her polite question. How did she and Joe go from midnight lovers to these sometimes hostile, sometimes carefully polite daytime enemies, she wondered. It was as if they were a real-life Psyche and Cupid. At night he came to her as her beautiful, sexy bridegroom, but during the day the lover disappeared almost as completely as Cupid had, and in the lover's place was this…this cold, rational attorney.

She got out three kinds of cheese and a loaf of sourdough bread and made him a grilled cheese sandwich, then retrieved the pitcher of sweetened iced tea from the refrigerator and poured them each a glass. Just about the time Joe had finished his sandwich and was drinking the last of his tea, the phone rang again.

Joe picked it up. He and Marcie stood, heads together as they listened.

"All right," Howard said. "Lemme talk to your pretty wife."

"She's here, standing right next to me."

"H-hello?" Marcie said.

"What's your name, woman? Marcella?"

"Marcie."

"Okay, *Marcie.* You listen close, because I ain't saying this but once. Old Joe found his way to Rhoda's house. He can show you how to get there. Once you're there at Rhoda's, I'll call you and tell you what to do next. You got that?"

Marcie looked at Joe, who nodded. "Yes. Yes, I've got it, but—"

"Joe, ol' buddy? You still there?"

"Yes," Joe said.

"You better stay home, if you know what's good for you and her and the kid. If you show up anywhere close I'll shoot you dead. I won't be shooting at yer feet or over your head like Rhoda likes to do. You got that?"

Marcie saw Joe's jaw tic. "Yes," he said gruffly.

"You sure?"

"I said yes."

"Okay. Miz Marcie, I need your cell phone. You and me, we're gonna handle this ourselves. Joe's out of it, you *capisce?* I'll call you, and when I do, I ain't gonna leave no message. Understand?"

"I've got it."

"Good. Now get this. You've got one hour and fifteen minutes to get to Rhoda's, once I hang up."

"Hang on," Joe said. "That's not enough time."

"It's gonna have to be, 'cause it's all you've got."

Joe shot Marcie a glance. "We need time to fill up the car."

"Aw, really? Well, in that case…" Howard said mockingly. "*What* did I tell you?" he yelled. "There ain't no *we,* Joe, ol' buddy, 'cause you ain't coming. Marcie? You'd better get going if you want to see the kid."

The line went dead.

Marcie looked at Joe, who stood there, the handset

clenched in his fist, his face stony. The muscle in his jaw quivered.

"Joe?"

He cut his gaze over at her. "I'm going with you."

"Oh, no, you're not," Marcie said firmly, fixing him with her sternest glare. "Did you not hear him? He will *shoot* you. If you don't believe him, I do, and I'll be damned if you're going to get yourself killed and not be here for Joshua and me."

He stared at her for a moment, as if she'd suddenly lapsed into an unknown language, then he blinked and looked down at the phone in his hand. He turned to put it into its cradle. When he turned back, his expression was harsh. "You listen to me. I'm not going to let you go out there by yourself. I'll be close by. So close that all you have to do is hit speed-dial one and I'll be there within two minutes. Understand?"

"You can't do that without him seeing you," she objected. "No. You can't, Joe. Listen to me. It's too dangerous."

"*You're* talking to *me* about dangerous?" He touched her cheek. "You are *not* doing this alone. I'll be close by. Call me. *Do you understand?*"

"Yes," she said, feeling the color drain from her face. "Don't you dare get yourself killed, Joe Powers. Don't you dare!"

Chapter Nine

Marcie ran upstairs to get a blanket and a coat to throw in the car just in case. When Marcie didn't come right back down, Joe went upstairs to check on her. She was standing in the hallway, a worried expression on her face. She had on jeans and was carrying her purse, a blanket and a coat.

"Got everything?" he asked.

"I don't know," she said, looking up at him. "I can't seem to get my thoughts together."

He gave her a little smile and held out his arms, not knowing whether she would be grateful or resentful that he wanted to comfort her. But she stepped forward and he pulled her into his embrace. "Do exactly what he says and remember, I'll be close." He lifted her chin with his finger. "Very close."

"What are you going to do?"

"Don't worry about that. You just concentrate on giving Howard the money and getting Joshua."

Her lip trembled at the mention of their son's name. She nodded.

Joe kissed her forehead, then handed her the satchel with the money in it. "Tell me which way you're going."

"We've been over that," she said.

"I know. Just tell me one more time, so we're both sure. My car needs gas, so I'm going to leave now and catch up with you on the road. You might not see me, but I'll be right behind you."

"Should I call you after he calls me?"

"No," he said quickly. "No. Don't call me. If Howard takes your phone away, he'll see that you called me and he'll assume you're telling me where you are. We can't take that chance. You just do what Howard tells you, and I'll keep up. I promise you I will."

She nodded, looking doubtful.

"Did you get that toy block you got from that house?"

"No. I forgot," she said, then gave him a small smile. "Thanks for reminding me. I know you think it's silly."

"I don't think it's silly at all. It's a connection to our child. Okay, then, you'd better grab that block. I've got to run. Marcie?" He looked into her eyes. She looked so frightened and so hopeful that it broke his heart. "Be careful." He turned to head down the stairs.

"Joe?"

He turned back.

"We will get him, won't we?"

He nodded and stepped close to her. He put his palms on both of her cheeks and kissed her lightly on the lips. "I swear to you we will." Then he turned and vaulted down the stairs. If his plan were going to work, he had only a couple of minutes to get ready.

WHEN ETHAN LEFT the Powerses' home, he didn't go far. He parked a block down the street, where he could watch the house without being seen. His cop's instincts and experience told him that he wouldn't have to wait long.

He thought about Joe Powers. From the moment his partner had shown him Joe's birth certificate, Ethan had felt a connection with the man who had been born within a month of Ethan himself. He figured he probably ought to be resentful of his grandfather for having a son and a grandson the same age. Instead, Ethan had been curious about Joe Powers, and now that curiosity was turned toward Powers's missing son.

Powers's front door opened and Joe emerged. He got into his car and drove away. That surprised Ethan. He'd figured the kidnapper would want Marcie to make the exchange. He debated following Joe, but the attorney hadn't looked as though he were headed for a ransom drop. He'd had nothing with him but his car keys. So Ethan continued to wait. Sure enough, within about one minute, Joe came walking through a neighbor's yard. After checking carefully to be sure no one was watching, he climbed into the trunk of the older vehicle.

Now *that* was interesting. Ethan perked up. He'd been right about the phone call. The exchange was this morning, and as he'd figured, the kidnapper had insisted that Marcie come alone to make the exchange. Joe had been warned not to go. Ethan understood Joe's need to be there to protect his wife and make sure the kidnapper hadn't harmed his son. It's what Ethan would have done. But those two facts didn't make Joe's plan any smarter or safer.

Ethan didn't have to wait five minutes before Marcie came out carrying a large purse and a large, obviously heavy tote. She passed by the trunk and opened the back right door and put the tote on the seat. Then she tossed her purse into the passenger seat. *Money.* The tote held money. There was a boxy shape to it that suggested stacks of bills. Ethan's heart raced. She was on her way to meet the kidnapper and, unbeknownst to her, her husband was hiding in the car's trunk, in the hopes of protecting her. Although Ethan understood Joe's motive, he couldn't even begin to fathom what Joe planned to do once Marcie got to the meeting place. He knew that climbing out of a car's trunk was a cumbersome process and he was dreadfully certain that if Joe tried to come to his wife's defense, he'd be dead or injured before he managed to get his feet on the ground.

That did it. Ethan had to follow them. Since he knew about the ransom call, he had an obligation to keep Marcie and Joe safe. As he pulled out behind her car, allowing enough room that she wouldn't notice that he was following her, his brain continued to process what he'd seen. They were going to need someone on their side to protect them against the kidnapper. He knew that it was possible to successfully exchange money for a kidnapped child or adult, but he had no idea what the percentages were. He certainly had no idea what the outcomes were when a family handled the exchange alone, without the help of the FBI or the police. All he knew was that he didn't want these new members of his family to be hurt or—worse—killed, because he didn't do his best to protect them.

Ethan dropped back a couple more car lengths from Marcie, which put him several blocks behind. He doubted seriously that she would notice him, but the kidnapper would be watching for a tail. And Ethan didn't want to be so close that the kidnapper could make him as a tail.

Before they even got as far as Kenner, Ethan's phone rang. He glanced at the dashboard, where the caller information was displayed on his car's Bluetooth. It was Dixon Lloyd, his partner.

"What's up, Dix. You know I took the day off, right?"

Dixon got straight to the point. "Our suspect in the household murder case just took a woman hostage," he said crisply.

"What?" Ethan wiped his face. "Damn it! Where?"

"Mercedes Boulevard."

"In Algiers? Listen, Dix, can you handle this by yourself? I'm—"

"No," Dixon said. "Even if I wanted to let you slide, the captain's demanding to know where you are. Said he didn't approve a day off."

Ethan muttered a few colorful words. "I left a message for him. He didn't call me back to tell me to come in."

"I'm just quoting him. He wants, and I quote, 'Delancey's butt out there at that house talking to that maniac *now!*'"

Ethan exited the interstate. "All right, I'm turning around. Where are you?"

"On my way there."

"Give me the address," he said.

Dixon recited it and Ethan tucked it into his memory. "Got it. I'm probably fifteen minutes away."

"Yeah, I'll be there in about nine minutes."

"See you," Ethan said, then punched the off button savagely, and cursed. He was abandoning Joe and Marcie, and he couldn't dispatch another officer in his stead. There would be too many questions. And talk about a blowup. If the captain found out that Ethan was planning to help with a kidnapping without reporting it first, he'd take possession of Ethan's badge by grabbing it through his butt.

He was still arguing with himself about whether he should reveal the kidnapping, when he got to the address Dixon had given him. Police cruisers and plain cars surrounded a pretty yellow house with blue shutters in the quiet neighborhood of Algiers. Two black vans were parked on the other side of the street and at least seven black-clad SWAT officers had rifles trained on the house.

Dixon saw him and waved him over.

"What's going on?" Ethan asked him in a whisper.

Dixon pointed to his phone. "Got him talking," he whispered, then turned his attention back to the phone. "No," he said patiently. "I've already told you, there's no way you're getting free passage out of here. Not a car and for damn sure not a plane. You're going to—" He winced and held the phone away from his ear and Ethan could hear a voice ranting and raving through the speaker.

"Sounds like you're doing great," he said to Dixon. "Why the hell did I have to bust my butt getting out here?"

Dixon raised his brow, shifted his gaze behind Ethan, then back as he continued talking to the killer who'd taken the woman hostage. "No, Donald, I haven't hung up on you and yes, I'm taking your demands *very* seriously," he said, just as the captain walked up next to Ethan.

"What the hell took you so long to get here, Delancey?"

BY THE TIME Marcie reached the road to Rhoda's house, it had started to rain. She turned on the windshield wipers and shivered, both from the damp chill in the air and from worry. She was already late. The rain was just going to make everything worse. The dirt-and-shell roads that wound through the swamps of south Louisiana could turn to gumbo within minutes in a rainstorm. Marcie had seen truck and ATV tires get so coated with the sticky stuff that their wheels would no longer turn.

Her phone rang, startling her. "Oh, no," she muttered. It was Howard. If he were watching the house, he knew she hadn't made it on time. She answered, her heart in her throat.

"Hey, Marcie," Howard said. "Where are you?"

She didn't want to lie, in case he could see her. "I'm close to Rhoda's house. I should be there in a few minutes."

"That means you're late. Well, I ain't got time to wait. Here's your instructions. Pay attention. You keep going on that same road until you come to a fork. There's a sign in the middle of the two roads. One side says Bayou DeChez. The other side don't say nothing. You take the fork without the sign. It's starting to rain, so watch your wheels. Don't run off the shoulder, else you'll get stuck. And trust me, woman, there ain't nobody gonna pull you out if you're that dumb. Keep going 'til you see a house on stilts. It's got a rusty metal roof and a blue door. You wait there."

"Wait?" Marcie cried, her heart sinking to her toes. "Why do I have to wait? How long? Will Joshua be there—?"

"Woman," Howard interrupted, "I told you, you don't get to ask questions. You better listen to me or you'll never get to see your kid. Now, you wait at that house and don't even think about going anywhere. I'll call you. Think you can handle that?"

Wait. She swallowed against the lump in her throat. "Yes," she said hoarsely. She knew that Joe was probably right and Howard was just a big coward and a bully who wanted people to pay attention to him. He liked running the show, so she needed to play up to him, because as far as her child was concerned, he *was* running the show.

The faint thread of hope that had kept her going for the past two years began to grow and strengthen. This was finally happening. If she did what Howard wanted her to, she would see Joshua soon. "Yes. I can handle it. When are you going to call back?"

Howard laughed. It was a gritty, ugly sound. "You

ask another question and this'll be the last time you ever hear my voice. Do you understand that?"

"Yes," she mumbled as despair warred with impatience inside her. "Yes. I understand," she said more loudly.

"It's started raining, so it'll get dark early. Don't slip off the road, 'cause if you get stuck in that swamp mud, it ain't going to be pretty. There a lot of gators."

"What if—?" Marcie cut off the question a split second before he hung up. She looked at her watch. It was almost two-thirty. His warnings ramped up the fear inside her to near panic. She was driving into the swamp alone in the rain in a car that didn't have four-wheel drive, carrying a bagful of cash and depending on the integrity of a man who was holding a two-year-old child for ransom.

She kept driving on down the road past Rhoda's house. The rain wasn't coming down hard, but that wasn't good news. It was one of those slow, steady rains that could last for days. The farther she drove, the longer the road in front of her seemed to stretch. The rain was creating a haze that hovered over the swamp on either side of the narrow road.

Finally, she came to the fork in the road. She had to park and get out to read the letters on the sign. Sure enough, the right-hand sign, block-printed with what looked like a Sharpie, was weathered and missing letters, but it was readable. BAYO_ DECHE_. The other sign might have had words on it at one time, but there was nothing recognizable there now.

Marcie got back into the car and took the left fork.

Her tires crunched on the broken oyster and mussel shells the highway department used in these parts to replace gravel on the narrow road. Just past the fork, she noticed a pile of broken electrical poles and wires on the side of the road.

Apprehension lodged in her chest. Obviously, they'd had electricity along this road at one time. But one of the hurricanes must have taken down the poles and nobody had ever replaced it. Thank God she'd brought a battery flashlight plus an emergency crank one.

Her tires slipped on the road that was getting muddier with every passing minute, and she crept along at a glacial speed. She prayed that it would stop raining and that no one else would try to drive out this way this afternoon. The road couldn't be more than fifteen feet wide and it dropped down at least a foot off each shoulder into murky water. She'd driven on some narrow roads in Louisiana, but never one this narrow. She had no idea what she would do if she met another vehicle. If the wheel of her car ever dropped off that edge, she'd be stuck.

Finally, she saw something dark looming over the right side of the road. The stilt house, maybe. She couldn't make out anything specific until she got much closer. When the structure began to take on shape and a little color, she saw how shabby it looked. There didn't appear to be anything underneath or behind it except murky swamp water. No boat and certainly no car, since there was obviously nowhere to pull off the road. The cabin itself was a crooked, wobbly thing that looked like it had been blown down during Katrina and set back upright by a careless, gigantic hand.

As she approached the house, Marcie carefully applied the brakes, but the tires slipped and the front of the car drifted slowly to the left. She compensated by turning the steering wheel, but it made no difference at all. A soft bump and the sudden dip in the front of the car told her that at least one wheel, possibly two, had gone over the shoulder. The car eased forward another inch, then stopped.

Marcie's throat was tight, her heart beating so hard and fast that she felt as though she couldn't breathe. She was frozen in place, afraid to move, worried that even the slightest shift of her body weight might send the car farther off the road until it nosedived into the muddy swamp.

For a long while she sat there, waiting to see if the car was going to slip any more. Finally, she decided that it either was or wasn't, but she would probably never know unless she moved. And she sure couldn't sit there all night...could she?

Marcie moved carefully, an inch or two at a time. Each time she moved an arm or leg, she stopped and held her breath, waiting to see if the car moved. She managed to slide out of the driver's seat and onto the center console without the car moving.

Now, all she had to do was get into the backseat and open the door and get out. She figured the hardest part was over, getting out from under the steering wheel and maneuvering over the gearshift on the console. She went into the backseat headfirst, rolling a bit so that she landed on her back. When she did, she felt an ominous shudder underneath her. The car was sliding.

Marcie froze, holding her breath until the steel frame quit moving. She took several deep breaths, then held her breath again, staying perfectly still. From what she could tell, the car seemed to have stabilized. So she eased the rear driver's side door open and climbed out. By the time she was standing on the muddy road, her legs felt like they were about to collapse and her whole body tingled from the adrenaline coursing through her veins. She looked up and down the road as far as she could see in the steady drizzle, which wasn't far, more than half afraid that Howard was watching, waiting to spring out and grab the money from her.

After squinting and staring in each direction, making sure she didn't detect any movement, she retrieved her purse from the passenger seat, then got the tote and the blanket from the backseat. Then she closed the doors as carefully as she could. But even for all her care, the car's frame groaned again.

She jumped backward. The vehicle gave another shudder, then slowly the front end dipped another several inches, placing the driver's side rear door right over a mud hole.

She stood there watching the back of the car for a few moments, fully expecting it to disappear, but it didn't move again. Looking up and down the muddy road, she crossed to the other side, walking as carefully as she could to avoid the deeper puddles. By the time she made it across the street and onto the narrow, rickety pier that led to the stairs, the soles of her tennis shoes were caked with sticky mud. She scraped the soles against the pier's rough wood until she'd gotten rid of most of it.

The stairs were wobbly, but much sturdier than the pier, although the soles of her shoes remained slippery. The weathered planks creaked in protest as she climbed, but nothing broke and she finally made it onto the small stoop. She'd estimated the height of the stilts with her eyes when she'd driven up. They looked to be about four feet above the level of the road. But now, looking down, it seemed as though the dark water was much farther below her. She carefully backed away from the edge of the porch and toward the door, almost tripping over a bucket that was about half-filled with rainwater. She shoved it out of the way with the toe of her shoe.

Her thoughts turned to Howard again. What if he were inside, waiting for her? What if he planned to ambush her inside the house, take the money and run? What if he didn't have Joshua and never intended to give her baby back to her. Marcie shivered and wiped rain out of her eyes. One thing was for certain—it was much too late to worry about whether Howard was inside the stilt house now. She was going inside because she had nowhere else to go.

When she pushed the door open and stepped inside, her hand automatically shot out to the right, patting the wall for a light switch, but there wasn't one. Her pulse began to race in the classic flight-or-fight adrenaline reaction. But still, she had to keep going. Otherwise she'd be out in the rain and probably catch hypothermia.

She remembered the pile of broken poles and wires

on the side of the road. Using the anemic sunlight that
crept in through the open door, she examined the in-
terior. It was a single room with two windows, one to
the left of the door and a second directly across from
it on the back wall.

Simple, thick curtains were pulled shut, shielding
enough light that it would be almost impossible to see
if she closed the door. She started toward the back window to open it, and something brushed across her face.
With a little cry, she swiped at it, imagining a huge spi-
der web or a bat. But her fingers touched a cool, small
chain hanging from the ceiling. It felt like the type of
ball chain that was used on lightbulbs and lamps.

She grabbed it and pulled, expecting nothing except a dry clicking sound. But a low-wattage lightbulb
on the ceiling flared, surprising her. How could there
be electricity? Then, just as the question formed in her
mind, she heard the low growl of a gas-powered generator starting up. Relief made her jaw ache, although
she hadn't realized she'd been clenching it.

The bulb was dim, but it helped a little as she sur-
veyed the room. To her profound relief, it was empty.
There was no one else here. Also, the little house felt
much tighter and more secure from the inside than it
had looked from the outside. Even so, she decided she
would stay toward the middle of the room and not press
her luck. While she was relatively sure that the one
hundred and twenty-five—okay, thirty—pounds on
her five-foot-eight-inch frame wouldn't tip the building
over, she wasn't going to take any chances.

She did tiptoe over to the back window long enough

to push the curtains aside. What greeted her was a pane of streaked, dusty glass, through which she could see the pale pink beginnings of sunset seeping through the rain clouds and shadowed by cypress trees draped in Spanish moss. In the dimming light, the trees looked like ghostly figures with tattered shawls.

The swamps of Lakes Pontchartrain and Maurepas were beautiful in a rugged, primitive way. The water, dark as mud, stretched out as far as the horizon, its vastness blocked only by clusters of cypress or tupelo trees and marsh grass. As she watched, a white heron flapped its wings then rose from the murky water and flew above the treetops, stirring a flock of seagulls that followed him. Their calls harmonized with the low groans and squeals of alligators as they splashed water while climbing onto a fallen log to sun, or slid back into the water after prey.

As beautiful and primitively elegant as the swamp was, the idea that sunset was not that far away made Marcie pull the curtains closed again. When it got dark, she didn't want anything out there looking in at her.

She swung the tote and her purse off her shoulder and set them on the floor near the door. Arching her shoulder and neck, she wondered just how much the hundred and seventy thousand dollars in twenties and hundreds weighed. From the furrow the heavy tote had made in her shoulder and the ache in her arms from hauling it up the stairs, she'd say forty pounds. Her purse was heavy, too, with the extra things she'd thrown in—the two flashlights, a couple bottles of water, a small package of toiletries and several protein bars. She looked at the bars ruefully. They weren't really appropriate for Joshua. As she was throwing things into her purse, it had hit her that everything she had was for a nine-month-old and Joshua was almost two and a half now. But surely, he could eat a protein bar.

Setting down the heavy bag, she fished the flashlight out and began exploring the small cabin. The walls were covered with what looked like canvas—or maybe burlap—that had been given one coat of white paint. The effect was spotty and oddly interesting, with an abstract pattern of light and dark that played over the walls like strange graffiti.

On the south wall, barely visible in pink light from the back window, was a counter on which sat an old-fashioned bowl and pitcher. Marcie lifted the pitcher. It was full of fresh water. There was no refrigerator or icebox, no cabinets and no food. Good thing she'd brought the protein bars.

She turned toward the other side of the room, the north side, directing the flashlight's beam into the shadows. The first thing she saw was a metal folding cot, its squatty legs about twelve inches off the floor. On it was a threadbare blanket, rolled up. Pushed up against the wall behind it was a small space heater. She studied it briefly, thinking that it looked about as dangerous as any electrical appliance she'd ever seen.

The heater coils on the front were exposed. The three metal safety guards were broken. It was plugged into an extension cord that ran across the floor, up the wall and out through the back window.

This corner was where she was supposed to sleep?

She glanced toward the front door, thinking she'd rather sleep in her car with the blanket over her and the doors locked, than to be in here alone, sleeping essentially on the floor with nothing but that ragged, moth-eaten piece of wool touching her.

Looking back at the space heater and thinking that it was certainly thoughtful of Howard to provide warmth on this rainy day, she noticed a smaller, darker cube next to it with a cord that was plugged into the same extension cord. Walking over and crouching down, she shone the flashlight and saw that it was a radio of some kind, probably a walkie-talkie.

She picked it up. There was a small green light on its top. Her hand jerked and she almost dropped it. It was on. Did that mean someone—Howard—had been here? Did it mean he was listening to her right now?

Marcie wiped her hands down her jeans as if she'd touched something dirty. She had no idea what the range of the walkie-talkies was, or precisely how to operate them. Still staring at it, she thought back over the past few minutes. Had she said anything out loud? Anything Howard could use against her? She didn't think so.

Standing, she turned on her heel and did her best to pretend that the walkie-talkie wasn't on and that there was no one on the other end of it. Still, she shuddered. Nothing about her exploration of the cabin had made her feel any better about where she was or how long she was going to be forced to stay. Howard hadn't even hinted at when he would contact her. All he'd told her was to wait in the cabin.

He—or someone—had obviously left the water

and the cot and blanket for her because she would be here overnight. The meanness of his threats contrasted sharply with the thoughtfulness of the comfort items he'd provided. Marcie wondered if the latter were Rhoda's idea, and how she'd managed to convince Howard to provide them.

Well, if Marcie was going to have to be here overnight, it wasn't going to be on that cot, covered by that moth-eaten rag folded on top of it. Thank goodness she'd brought in her clean, fresh blanket. She could cover up with it, although she had little hope of sleeping a wink in this rickety cabin that only had one way in or out through a flimsy, hollow door.

Marcie wiped her face and did her best not to give in to the tears that were hovering just behind her eyes. Now that she was here alone in this grubby little hovel in this awful swamp that had practically devoured her car, it was getting harder and harder to believe that all this was going to lead her to her little boy. It felt like a wild-goose chase. All the horror stories she'd ever heard about kidnappings gone wrong swirled in her mind.

Despite her determination, her eyes stung and filled with tears. The tears spilled over her eyelids and ran down her cheeks. She knew what she needed. She needed Joe. If she could hear his low, reassuring voice pointing out all the odds that were in their favor, she'd calm down.

Then what he'd told her came rushing back to her memory. He'd promised her that he'd be close by, that all she had to do was call and he'd come to her rescue. But if that were true, why hadn't he rushed to her aid when the car slid into the swamp? Had he watched and decided that she wasn't in danger? Or had he been worried that Howard might be close by and didn't want to expose himself?

She wanted to call him, even though he'd told her not to. She knew it was a precaution to keep Howard from thinking she'd passed along her location. But she was terrified that if she didn't talk to him, she was going to have a full-blown panic attack. She hadn't had one of those since those first weeks after Joshua was taken, but she could feel the telltale symptoms starting. She could already feel her heart rate increasing.

She dug her phone out of her pocket and entered speed-dial one. Her fingers tightened around the phone as she heard the first ring. But it cut off in the middle. Pulling the phone away from her ear, she looked at the display. *No service.*

"No!" she cried. She shook the phone, as if that would help, then punched speed-dial one again. "Hello?" she cried into the speaker. "Hello!" Louder this time. "Joe? Hello? Please?" But the phone was dead. No sound. No service.

She held the phone high, then low, walked over to the back window and along the back wall, but no matter what she tried—checking voice mail, dialing a number, sending a text, even trying to access her email—it still indicated no service. Growling in frustration, she suppressed a sudden desire to fling the device at the wall. But, before she gave up, she wanted to try the phone outside in the open air. So she stepped outside onto the little stoop and tried her phone again. Still nothing. She looked around. Was she crazy to think that if she walked a few yards up or down the road, or got out from under the canopy of cypress branches, she might have more luck?

She started down the stairs, holding on to the rickety rail with one hand while continuing to check the phone with the other. Halfway down, she stopped, too frustrated and deflated to continue. Of course there was no cell service. Otherwise, why would Howard have left a walkie-talkie set up and charged and ready to use in the house?

She and Joe should have known that. What a stupid, dangerous game they were playing. They never should have bought in to Howard's threats. Never should have talked to him on their own. It was a mistake not to go to the police. No matter how many times she'd cried wolf in the past about seeing Joshua, the police were obligated to respond to a kidnapping or a child abduction. They'd have to help them. It was their job.

Marcie looked down at her car, submerged halfway up its front wheels. She had no idea where Joe was, if he'd managed to follow her at all. There was nothing she could do except wait. She thought for a moment about abandoning the money and heading back the way she'd come on foot. Eventually she'd find Joe or someone else.

But it was still raining, and the pink glow that had filtered through the clouds from the west was fading to a deep purple. It would be dark in no time. She had the flashlights, but how much good would they do if the rain increased. It terrified her to think that she might misstep and fall into the murky waters of the Maurepas swamp.

Feeling as old as Methuselah, she stood and climbed slowly back up the stairs. As she reached for the doorknob, a banshee's screech wailed from inside the shack.

Chapter Ten

Marcie let out a startled shriek a split second before her brain identified the screeching as the walkie-talkie. She approached the device with a level of dread and horror worthy of encountering an alien. When she picked it up, static made it vibrate in her hand.

"Marcie?" a scratchy, staticky voice said. It was Howard. It had to be.

She cleared her throat, took a deep breath and, trying to sound strong and confident, said, "H-Howard?" She grimaced. Her voice was as tentative and squeaky as a terrified little girl's.

"So you made it." Howard's slimy voice oozed through the speaker.

Marcie shuddered with dread. "Where…are you?"

He laughed. "You'll know soon enough. Point is, I know exactly where you are and what you've been doing."

Marcie glanced up and shone her flashlight into the corners and along the roofline. Did he have some kind of cameras set up? Was he watching her now? She didn't care, didn't have time to worry about his scare tactics. She wanted Joshua.

"Where do we meet?" she demanded, her voice more authoritative now. "And how soon? I want to get my child and get out of here."

"Now you know you can't do that, Marcie. Not with your car like it is."

"You know— Where are you? Is Joshua with you?" Marcie's anger ignited like the fuse on a stick of dynamite. "I have your damned money. Give me my baby!" She stalked over to the door and looked out. "Where. Are. You?"

"You sure are bossy, considering." He laughed.

"Just tell me where he is. That's all I want to know."

"Don't you worry. Rhoda's taking good care of him. She's all smitten with him for some strange reason. Poopy diapers and runny nose and all."

"Howard!" Marcie growled through clenched teeth. "I want my child—now."

"Soon enough. Soon enough. First, I'm going to have some fun."

Terror flashed through her like a lightning bolt, sending tingling fear all the way to her fingers and toes. "Fun?" she repeated weakly.

He didn't answer. Marcie looked out the door again, and saw an old, dirty green pickup approaching from the same direction she'd come from.

"Howard?"

"There you are," Howard said. He stuck an arm out the window and waved at her. "Wave back. Say hi."

The truck was loud. She couldn't believe she hadn't

heard it, but there it was, lumbering up the muddy road, with Howard at the wheel. He waved again, then honked his horn. The earsplitting sound made her nearly jump out of her skin.

Then it hit her. The truck. The exchange. Maybe he had Joshua! She ran out the door and started down the stairs, her terror forgotten. She could deal with whatever Howard had planned for her, as long as she got her little boy back.

Her foot slipped on a step and she almost fell, but she caught herself on the flimsy rail. Suddenly out of breath, she stopped and regrouped. She had to be careful. She had to stay safe and sound for her baby. Before she got halfway down the stairs, the horn honked again. She stopped and looked over the rail. Howard gunned the engine and he rammed the pickup into the rear fender of her car. The car's back end twisted until it was almost perpendicular to the road. As she watched, stunned, he backed up, shifted gears with a metallic groan, then rammed her car again. The impact didn't do much damage to the bumper, but it forced the car a little farther off the road. From Marcie's vantage point it looked as though it would nosedive into the swampy water any second.

She shook herself. *Joshua!* What if he was in the truck? Was he safe? Was he in a safety seat? Dear God, what if he wasn't? He could be hurt by the collisions.

"Joshua!" she cried. "Howard! Where's Joshua?" She rushed down the stairs, trying to see inside the truck, but couldn't see anyone else. "Howard! Do you have Joshua?"

But Howard was gunning the engine and didn't hear her. She remembered she was still holding the walkie-talkie, so she pressed the button.

"Where's Joshua?" she cried. "Where is my son?" She ran down a few more steps, just as her car groaned and moved slowly forward. Howard gunned the truck's engine again.

"No, wait!" she cried, reaching the bottom step and running across the pier to the road.

The truck's gears ground loudly as Howard shifted into first. Marcie was almost across the road when he pulled forward, spraying mud. She kept running as he eased past her car without so much as tapping the fender and sped up. She was parallel with the passenger door, but still an arm's length away, when he passed her.

"Hey, Marcie!" Howard yelled into the walkie-talkie and waved out the window at her again. She stopped pumping her arms and legs and struggled to breathe as she whispered to herself over and over again, "He doesn't have Joshua. He doesn't have him. Rhoda wouldn't let him take the child without her." She swallowed. "He doesn't have him."

She stood in the middle of the muddy road, her chest heaving with its efforts to get enough oxygen as the truck headed deeper into the bayou, away from civilization. As he disappeared from view, Howard waved one last time.

She watched the truck's tail until it disappeared around a bend and the sound of its motor faded. He would come back. She knew it. But the minutes passed, the sun went down and the sky began to darken, and all she heard were the calls of birds as they settled down, the occasional moan of an alligator and the whispers of the evening breeze rustling the leaves.

As dusk stole color from the world and turned everything gray, she turned around and trudged back to the house. She looked at her car. Now the car was facing the opposite direction and the wheels were totally submerged in the murky water. She couldn't see the right front tire at all.

She'd already decided that there was no way of getting the car back on the road, but now, after watching Howard ram it again and again, and knowing that he could have stopped the truck at any moment and confronted her, panic crawled up the back of her throat. Maybe she hadn't abandoned all hope of getting her car back on the road. But now, she knew it was hopeless. She was stuck in this death trap of a cabin, on this deserted road, stranded and helpless. The promise that Joe had made to her, that he would be close by in case anything happened, was fading as fast as her belief that she would ever see her child again.

It was truly dark now, and the relaxing, tranquil sounds of the swamp during the day were turning ominous. The quiet groans of the alligators now echoed through the darkness like moaning ghosts. The bird calls that were interesting and beautiful during the daytime now sounded predatory.

Marcie wasn't sure she had the strength to climb back up the stairs to the house. She finally made it, though. When she slammed the door, she examined it for a lock. There was a laughably ineffective push lock in the knob. She tested it to see if it worked. It did, but Marcie knew that even she, as tired as she was, could kick it in with scarcely any effort.

She looked down at herself. She was soaked and the bottoms of her jeans and her tennis shoes were covered with mud. To her surprise, she still held the walkie-talkie in her hand and the little green light was still on. She was tempted to press the talk button and vent all her fear and frustration and anger at Howard by screaming and cursing at him. But all that would do was make her sick, and if Howard was anywhere near Joshua, he'd hear her. She didn't want that to be his first introduction to her. She put the walkie-talkie back on its charger and stood there staring at it, not really thinking of anything, for a long time.

Wet droplets drizzling down her back and numbness in her toes reminded her that she was wet and getting colder by the moment. If she were going to be able to rest at all, she had to dry off somehow. She hadn't brought a change of clothes, because she hadn't thought about being stranded or caught in the rain.

After taking off the mud-caked shoes, she stripped off her wet jeans and set them aside. With all the rain, the bucket that was sitting on the stoop might be three-quarters full by now. She went outside, shivering in her wet wool peacoat and underwear, and quickly rinsed out the jeans and cleaned as much mud as she could off her tennis shoes. It was no longer raining, although at this point that didn't mean much. The road was impassible, her car was out of commission and she was already soaked.

Back inside, she tested the space heater to see if it worked. It did. She twisted the knob until it clicked twice. Sure enough, the wires began to turn orange and she heard a fan kick on, blowing warm air her way. Turning the cot onto its side, she used it as a drying rack, hanging her coat and jeans on it and setting her tennis shoes in front of it. For a moment, she stood in front of the heater, shivering as the warm air drifted across her chilled skin. She chafed her arms and held out one foot and then the other to the heat, until her toes began to tingle as the numbness faded.

Looking at the pink wool blanket she'd brought with her, she considered whether she had the nerve to strip completely. She was already barefoot, with nothing on her lower half but her panties. If anyone—and by anyone she meant Howard—forced their way into the house, she'd hardly be any more vulnerable wrapped in a blanket than she was right now. She still had nothing to use as a weapon.

Weapon. "Oh, my God," she whispered. She'd completely forgotten that after Joe had moved out, she'd bought a small can of pepper spray to keep in her purse, for those times when she came home late at night. Or when being alone in that big house, without him or Joshua, made her feel exposed and helpless. She went over to her purse and dug down in it until her fingers closed around the cylindrical shape of the pepper spray. Pulling it out, she examined it with the flashlight. It was a narrow spray can about four inches long. The spray button was on the top and it had a wristband for easy carrying. She slipped it over her wrist. At least now she wasn't totally helpless. If Howard tried to attack or hurt her, an eyeful of the spray might stop him.

Letting the spray can dangle by her wrist, she grabbed a protein bar and one of the water bottles she'd stowed in her purse, and sat over by the space heater. Then she peeled off her damp sweater and her silk undershirt and draped them over the upturned cot.

Soon she was warm and cozy in her pink wool blanket and sitting in front of the fire. She drank half the water in one long swallow, then chewed a couple of bites of the protein bar. It wasn't the tastiest supper she'd ever had by a long shot, but she could feel the bar hit her stomach and figured that by morning she'd be glad she'd eaten it.

By the time she finished, she could barely keep her eyes open and her muscles and joints were aching. At least her feet had finally warmed up. Not wanting to take down her makeshift drying rack, she left the cot where it was and lay down on the floor. She eyed the ratty wool blanket that had been provided for her, but immediately rejected it.

She dragged her purse and the tote bag full of money over near her, and then wrapped up in the blanket like a mummy, using her purse for a pillow. She closed her tired eyes, but after a few minutes, she had to give up. She couldn't go to sleep. Her mind was racing too fast. The events of the past few days ran amok in her head.

Joe, looking irritated and grim when he'd opened the door of his apartment to her—had that been a few days ago? The detective standing next to Joe in their living room, both of them acting as if they had no idea how much they looked alike. The little wooden table and chairs in Rhoda's house, and the small blackboard with the name *Joshy* written on it. The blue-and-white plastic block she'd picked up, with the *J* in red on one side and an image of a little boy on the other. Her child, her little Joshua, with his wide dark eyes and the little widow's peak in the center of his forehead, in the child seat in the back of the Nissan.

Sighing, she turned over and scooted just a little closer to the heater, then closed her eyes again. She started singing "Danny Boy" in her head, her usual lullaby that worked better than anything else to help her fall asleep. But soon, her back, facing away from the heater, was getting chilly. She wondered if it would hurt to turn the thermostat up to high. Maybe she'd do that. She pulled her knees up to her chest and stuck her hands inside the folds of the blanket. After a while, if she were still cold. She shrugged her shoulders and tried to relax, then tucked her chin into the blanket and began humming "Danny Boy" again.

She heard a noise.

She didn't realize she'd been asleep until she jerked awake. What was that? She lifted her head and felt the heater on her face.

She heard it again. It sounded like someone—or something—was scratching around the foot of the stairs. *Howard!* Her pulse hammered in her temples. She grabbed her cell phone and started punching in 911 before she remembered that there was no service out here. Still, she looked at the display optimistically.

It still said *no service.* She tried speed-dial one, tried texting, even tried 911 again. But nothing happened.

In a few seconds, she heard the noise a third time. It was fainter, as if the creature making it were moving away. Or had realized they were making noise and were trying to be quiet. No animal would do that, would they? She could almost hear Joe's rational voice in her head. *Sure, if they were being chased by a predator.*

Somehow she didn't think the creature down there would be classified as prey. As soon as that thought crossed her mind, she deliberately dismissed it.

And surely it wasn't Howard. Why would he bother to sneak? He hadn't been cautious this afternoon. No, he would probably walk right up the stairs, clomping in heavy shoes on every step, and push the door in, because that tiny lock on the doorknob wouldn't keep out a raccoon, much less a man who looked like he topped two hundred pounds easily. With that thought in her head, she began imagining that the scratching and rustling were actually the creaking of the stairs as someone crept up them.

As quietly as she could, she pushed herself to her feet and reached for her undershirt and sweater. She pulled them over her head, breathing as carefully and steadily as she could so she could keep listening. She slipped on her tennis shoes and her coat, leaving the jeans, because they'd be much too hard to put on, especially quietly.

Still aware of the rustling and scratching, she moved silently around the cabin, watching the display on her phone. She wasn't even sure why she was still trying. It was obviously a waste of time. Still, what did it hurt? Maybe somewhere, in an awkward corner or arm's length out a window, she might conceivably pick up one bar and manage to dial 911, or Joe. Staring at the display, she wandered close to the door and once again stood still, barely breathing. Listening.

Had the noise stopped? She didn't hear it anymore. Maybe whatever it was had given up and gone away. Holding her breath, she stood like a statue. She heard what sounded like the click of claws on wood, getting fainter with each second that passed. She forced a small, quiet laugh. It probably *was* a raccoon. Luckily it hadn't climbed the stairs and somehow pushed the door open using its little prehensile fingers. She'd have probably fainted.

After another minute of waiting and listening, Marcie still didn't hear anything. She should go back to bed and try to sleep as much as possible, or she would be exhausted in the morning. But she was too hyper now. There was no way she could get to sleep.

She looked at her phone. It was ridiculous that she couldn't pick up a signal somewhere. She was worried about Joe. About what had happened that kept him from showing up. He'd told her he'd be there within minutes, if she called him. Maybe he was just far back enough toward town that he could pick up a signal on his phone and therefore he didn't realize that she couldn't. Maybe he was still waiting for her to call.

Hadn't he told her once that phone signals might be stronger at night than during the day? Or was that radio signals? She couldn't remember, but if he were out there waiting for her call, she had to try and see if she could find at least one bar. It made sense that there might be a better chance at night, didn't it? There probably were fewer phone calls being made, fewer internet connections being used.

She started to unlock the door but she paused, thinking of the noise she'd heard. "Come on, Marcie," she whispered to herself. She hadn't been afraid of the swamp in the daytime. There shouldn't be anything to fear at night. It was the same swamp with the same wildlife. And all she wanted to do was step out onto the stoop and check her phone. It wasn't as if she were going down the stairs.

She took a deep breath, then turned the lock and stepped out onto the porch, a little surprised at how dark it was. The moon wasn't up yet and although the sky was clear and the stars were bright, the cypress trees and Spanish moss draped the bayou with shadows. The night was quiet, nothing but rainwater dripping and the breeze stirring the leaves. Was it a sleepy, all-the-animals-are-happy silence? She didn't think so. It seemed to her that the air was laden with caution, as if the wildlife were holding their breaths.

Marcie glanced at the phone's display. Still no signal. With a frustrated sigh and a stinging of her eyelids, she stuck the phone into the pocket of her coat. Maybe she'd go back inside and wrestle on her jeans, then go down to the pier, or maybe all the way to the road, and check the phone again. As she felt behind her for the doorknob, she heard the same rustling sound.

She froze. Her first thought was Howard. Shock burned through her nerve endings as her body tensed.

Was she scaring herself? After all, the stairs creaked whenever a slight breeze stirred. Nothing could climb up here without making a lot more noise than she'd heard.

Still, she put her finger on the pepper spray can button, then whirled, prepared to drench whatever was behind her. But before she'd stopped spinning, powerful arms grabbed her and shoved her against the rough board wall of the cabin.

Chapter Eleven

With a yelp, Marcie tried to throw herself sideways, hoping her momentum didn't send her plummeting over the railing or down the stairs. She managed to hit the button on the pepper spray can, but the shot of spray was deflected by the shadowy figure's arm. He clamped an ironlike hand over her mouth. She gasped and tried to scream, but the hand was too strong. Tried to bite him but her lips were pressed too tightly against her teeth.

"No!" she tried to cry. Nothing but a muffled groan came from her throat. *No!* He would not overpower her. She'd throw herself over the rail first. She struggled with all her strength, pushing, kicking, trying to bite. She sucked in air to try one more time to scream and caught a whiff of a familiar scent. A pleasant, poignant mixture of soap, citrus and clean cotton. At the same time she heard a low voice urging her to stop struggling. The combination stopped her cold.

Joe? Her fingertips tingled even as her limbs went limp with relief.

"Marcie," he whispered urgently. "Stop wiggling. You're going to send us right over the edge."

She gasped again, but the only noise she made through his hand was a mumble.

"Shh! Marcie. It's Joe."

"Mm-mmmph," she groaned, which sounded nothing like *I know.*

Joe pulled her inside and kicked the door closed. "Are you going to be quiet?" he muttered.

"Mmm-hmm, mmm mmm," she said. *Of course I am.* She nodded again.

He let go of her and took his hand away from her mouth.

"Joe? Wh-what are you—?" she cried, her hand over her heart. "You scared me almost totally to death!"

"Sorry," he muttered. "Are you okay?"

She licked her lips and tasted blood. "Ow." When she touched her finger to the sore place, it came away red. "I bit my lip."

"Yeah," he said. "Trying to bite me."

"What are you doing here—?" But before she finished speaking the full realization of what it meant to have Joe right here, right in front of her, hit her and she flung herself into his arms. "Oh, my God, oh, my God, Joe! You're here!" She wrapped her arms around his waist and hugged him as tightly as she could.

"Please, don't let this be a dream," she said as her eyes filled with tears and her voice turned thick with emotion.

"Hey," he said, pulling her tightly into his embrace. "It's no dream. I'm here. I'm right here."

For a moment, she just held on to him and relished the feel of his strong arms around her. She buried her nose in his shirt, seeking that little hollow just under his collarbone. He smelled so good. Like soap and clean shirts. Like Joe.

Then reality pushed its way into the middle of her joy and relief. "Joe, no! You can't be here. You have to leave. Howard said he'd— If he finds out you're here, he'll hurt Joshua. We can't—" She tried to swallow around a sudden lump in her throat. "We can't let him cut our baby's finger off. You've got to get out of here!"

"Hey, shh." Joe held on to her, wrapping his arms around her and holding her so close she could feel his heart beating. "It's going to be okay."

"Wait! Wait a minute." She lifted her head and felt cool air on her cheeks. She realized they were wet with tears. "We've been so stupid. We can't stay here and wait for that horrible man. We've got to get out of here and call the police. I don't care what they said about me. They have to help us. It's their job, right? They've got to. We can't do this on our own. Joe, I'm so scared."

"I know," he whispered, his voice muffled because he was pressing his nose into her hair. "I'm scared, too." His embrace tightened and she heard him take a shaky breath.

"What's the matter?" she asked, peering at him in the darkness.

She felt his spine go rigid.

"Joe? What is it?"

"We can't leave, Marcie."

"What do you mean? Why not? Where did you park your car?"

He let go of her and his gaze met hers. His expression was grim. "I don't have a car. I hid in your trunk."

"You hid—?" She laughed uneasily. "In the trunk of my car? I can't believe I didn't know you were in there."

He nodded. "Hah. There could be cats fighting in the trunk and you wouldn't open it. I knew I'd be safe there."

"I don't like trying to open the trunk with an armload of stuff. It's much easier to throw the bags in the backseat." She smiled at him. "I can't believe you're here."

"I wasn't going to let you come out here alone, no matter what Howard said."

"You said you had to get gas. That you'd catch up with me."

He shrugged, then winced. "I'm sorry for not telling you the truth. I considered following you in the other car, but I decided that would be too obvious. Howard would be sure to spot it. I doubt many strangers drive out this far."

"I couldn't believe I was on a road. It's so narrow. I was afraid the car was going to go over the edge any second. And then it did."

"So I figured the only thing I could do was hide in the trunk and wait until it got dark to get out." He rubbed his shoulder. "I didn't expect to be rammed by a truck."

"Oh, Joe. You were in the trunk when Howard rammed the car. Are you all right?"

"A little sore from being knocked around, but nothing serious. There's actually a lot of buffer in your bumper."

"That's good to know," she said wryly. "How did you do it? I didn't see your car when I left the house."

"I put it into the garage and closed the door manually."

She couldn't decide if she was more thrilled to see him, or more angry that he hadn't told her what he was going to do. "But why didn't you tell me? You didn't have to ride in the trunk the whole way. We could have stopped along the way to let you get into the car."

Joe shook his head. "Nope. I didn't want to put that kind of pressure on you. If you knew I was in the trunk and Howard confronted you or started asking you questions, I didn't want you to have to lie to him. If you didn't know I was there, you wouldn't have to worry about anything but the truth as you knew it."

Marcie looked at her husband, the man she'd accused of not caring for their son as much as she did. The man she'd resented for moving on with his life, instead of wallowing in the loss of the child they'd made together. She'd never thought of him as particularly courageous, never really thought about that at all. He was just a man, a man she'd fallen in love with. A man who had been scarred by an unstable childhood and a mother who was most kindly described as a stripper. But now, looking at him with his hair tousled and his shirt wrinkled, she thought she was beginning to see the kind of man he really was.

She doubted he'd ever forgive her for the things she'd said to him when she was hurting so badly that nothing he or anyone did could ease her grief and pain. He'd put up with more from her than any husband, much less a husband who had lost a child, should have to.

Every time she'd gone to him with a crazy story of having seen Joshua, he'd supported her. Even this last time. And he hadn't done it to placate her, she knew, but because, even after she'd cried wolf so many times, he still believed she might have actually seen Joshua.

If—no, when—they got Joshua back, what then? Joe wouldn't come back to her, she was sure about that. She'd destroyed any hope that he could look past the way she'd treated him. But he'd be there for his son. She didn't doubt that for one instant. Maybe not every day, but he'd be there.

Of all the things she didn't know about her husband, she did know one thing for sure. He loved his son more than anything in the world. He would do anything, even sacrifice his life, for their son. Maybe someday, far enough in the future that the wounds she'd inflicted on him had healed, he would be willing to try again to be a family. To be three once more.

Joe watched Marcie, becoming more worried about her by the second. She'd been staring at nothing for several moments. "Hon? Are you okay?" he asked. Was she angry at him for lying to her?

"What?" Marcie blinked several times then looked at him. "I can't believe you did that. It was a brave thing to do. And—" she took a breath "—you could have been hurt really badly if Howard had rammed the car any harder."

"So Howard drove by, banged into the car a few times to be sure you couldn't drive it, then just drove away? Did he talk to you at all? Did he give you any information about the swap?"

"No," she said. "When I saw his pickup, the only thing I could think about was Joshua. At first I was sure Howard had him with him, that he was there to make the exchange. But then he rammed into the car, and all I could think about was that Joshua might be in that truck. I was terrified. Was he in there, not in a child seat? Was Howard just letting my baby bounce around in there? I ran down there, but he just took off, spraying mud everywhere."

"I could hear you yelling, and I figured the other voice I heard was Howard's, but I couldn't make out what you were saying. So he didn't give you any information about when we could make the swap?"

She crossed her arms. "He never got out of the pickup, and I'm glad he didn't. He's awfully creepy." She shivered. "Oh, Joe, I've been so scared."

"I know, hon," he said. He held out his arms for her. He expected her to hesitate but she didn't. She stepped right into his embrace. As he pulled her close and breathed in the familiar scent of her hair, he asked himself what kind of idiot had he been to leave her? He should have had enough patience, enough love in him, to stay with her through the worst of her grief. Instead, he'd told himself that she was better off without him. That she'd heal faster without him around to remind her that *he* had let their child be stolen.

He'd been so wrong. He'd convinced himself that he'd done it for her. That moving out and going to work for NCMEC were for her. Now he knew better. He'd been running away.

And now, if he couldn't get their little boy back, he'd be a coward and a failure. Even if they got Joshua back, Marcie would never trust him around their son again. Not that she'd refuse to let him see him. She wasn't cruel. But trust—no. It would take more than a lifetime to earn her trust again.

He pressed his nose into her sweet-smelling hair and tried to blink away the stinging behind his eyes.

"What do we do now?" she asked.

He took a deep breath, then lifted his head. "I think we try to sleep. It's been a very long day and tomorrow is going to be longer. You need to try to get some sleep." He glanced around and saw the cot upturned with her clothes on it. Then he set her away from him and looked her up and down. "I take it your clothes got wet? That's why you have no pants on?"

She looked down at herself. "Oh. I forgot." She shivered and glanced at the cot. "I doubt my jeans are dry yet. Can you believe this place has electricity—and a heater? Howard has provided us with all the comforts of home."

"I can't believe it hasn't burned down. That heater is dangerous. The safety guard is gone. I'm not so sure it's a good idea to leave it on."

Marcie shivered. "But it's getting colder," she said. "What do you think the temperature is outside? Like thirty?"

Joe laughed. "No. More like fifty. Maybe a little lower."

"Really? I'm freezing."

"I'm going to get the clothes off the cot so you can sleep on it. I'll lie beside you. Then if Howard or an alligator shows up, I'll be between you and the door."

"An alligator? Really?" A tiny smile lit her face and his heart began to pound. Her smile was so beautiful.

Shrugging, he smiled back at her. Then she surprised him by hugging him again.

"Thank you for hiding in the trunk," she whispered.

"No problem," he said, still trying to keep it light. He figured she'd push away from him any minute now. That was probably a good thing because holding her was becoming one of his favorite things—again. But she didn't. Instead, her arms tightened around his waist, sending a surge of desire through him that was both pleasant and painful. He gritted his teeth, trying to quell the inevitable reaction of his body. It worked—kind of.

Finally, she stirred and stepped backward. Joe let her go.

"I'm not sure why they have electricity anyhow. There's only one light—one bulb—and that space heater. Nothing else. Not a coffeepot or a toaster or anything."

"This is obviously a fishing camp. Maybe they bring that stuff with them."

Just then there was a buzzing, then a click that sounded like it came from the generator outside. The heater clicked, too, then the coils began to fade to black.

Marcie gasped and clutched his arm. "Somebody cut off the generator," she said, worried. "Do you think it's Howard?"

"No," he said, stepping over to the window.

"But what if it *is* him?"

Joe parted the curtains slightly and looked down. "Nobody out there. I think it sounded like a timer, cutting off. Looks like that's all the warmth we're going to get tonight. Let's get you tucked into that cot before the little bit of heat we've got totally dissipates."

"I don't think sleeping in that cot off the floor is going to be very warm. What if we both slept on the floor?"

He glanced at her but she wasn't looking directly at him.

"Would that work?" she asked. "Could we keep warm if we snuggled together?"

Joe didn't even have to think about it. He'd be warm all right. Too warm. And with his wife's exquisitely sexy body pressed tightly against him, he wouldn't sleep a wink.

JOE HAD MANAGED to maneuver so that Marcie was spooned against his back, but the fact that his front wasn't pressed against her hadn't made as much difference as he'd hoped it would. Maybe his arousal wasn't pressed up against her, but her breasts were against his back and her upper thighs were pressed against his butt. He found it as hard to get to sleep lying like this as he'd figured it would be facing the other direction.

Finally he'd started to drift off, only to hear Marcie's quiet murmur close to his ears.

"Joe? What's going to happen tomorrow?"

"Hmm?" he said, still half-asleep.

"Tomorrow. What are we going to do? Hand over the money and hope that Howard keeps his word?"

"I don't see how we can do anything else. We came here in good faith, with as much money as we could get together." He yawned. "I suppose we've got to believe that Howard will be acting in good faith, too."

"That's what bothers me. You told me that you think Rhoda really loves Joshua. I think so, too. Look at everything she was doing for him—teaching him, taking care of him. I'll bet there's no way he can convince her to give him up."

Joe didn't know how to answer Marcie. She'd echoed his very thoughts. He tried to think of something to say to reassure her but he was acutely aware of the silence stretching out.

"You don't think we're going to get him back, do y—?" Her voice broke. "Oh, Joe, I don't know if I can live if we don't get our baby back."

Joe turned over and sat up, leaning back against the rough plank wall of the house. "I don't know, Marcie. I wish I did. I wish I could say that I'm sure everything will go just as we planned tomorrow. My fear is that, while Howard may have thought up the blackmail scheme, Rhoda's really the brains of that outfit. But if Rhoda is behind this, she may have a plan to take the money and run."

Marcie sat up, too, and pulled her knees up to her chin and wrapped her arms around them. "I'm so scared," she said, starting to cry. "My little boy. What will I do if I never see him again? What will I do?"

Joe put his arm around her but she remained stiff

and unyielding. Her shoulders shook as she cried silently. He wished he could do something to make her feel better. Wished he could reassure her, but whether it was Howard or Rhoda running the show, he didn't believe for one minute that they were planning to give Joshua back to them.

He kept his arm around her, kept patting her arm and murmuring to her. He didn't know how to make her feel better. He never had. He'd failed at comforting her after Joshua was taken. He'd been too consumed with guilt then. The job with the NCMEC had helped, but he still carried around plenty of guilt and it still weighed him down, keeping him from being able to lift up Marcie.

He had to do something, but what? He had no idea. All he knew was that he'd give anything, even his life, to put their child back into her arms. To that end, he had to come up with a plan to counter Howard's.

After a long time, Marcie's sobs quieted, her shoulders stopped shaking and she laid her head against his chest. He figured she was asleep, and he pressed his cheek against her hair and closed his eyes.

After a few minutes, she spoke. "Joe?"

"Hmm?"

"Thank you for hiding in the trunk."

"You already thanked me for that," Joe said.

"Well, it's worth two. It was a very brave thing to do."

"No, it wasn't," he said. "You're the brave one. You drove out here to confront Howard all by yourself."

"But that's just it. I wasn't by myself. You promised me you'd be here when I needed you, and you were."

He pressed a kiss to her temple, wishing he were as brave as she made him sound.

They sat in silence for a while, watching the orange coils on the space heater. After several minutes, Marcie spoke. "Tomorrow, if everything goes well, we'll have our baby back." She sighed. "What then?" she asked in a trembling voice. "When we get Joshua back? What then?"

"What do you mean?" he asked.

"How...will we handle that?"

"You mean Joshua? We'll just have to do everything we can to help him. He'll grieve for Rhoda, of course. And it will take a while for him to learn to trust us. We've got the resources of the center that we can use. There are a couple of really good child psychologists we refer reunited families to, and—"

"Joe," she interrupted, sitting up straight. "I know you have the knowledge and the resources to do all the right things for Joshua. I'm talking about us—the three of us."

He had no idea what she wanted him to say. What he'd like to say was, *We'll all be together and we can get on with being a family, like we were before. We can be three again.* But that wasn't his call. It was hers. She'd never had a problem expressing her opinion, so if that was what she wanted, she'd tell him.

No, this was a deeper question. They both knew that they'd been drifting apart since before Joshua was born. Trouble was, he wasn't sure why. "The most important thing is to be there for him. Once we make sure we can do that, then we'll see."

Marcie heard the hesitation in Joe's voice and understood exactly what was bothering him. She'd said horrible things, unforgiveable things, to him. She'd even told him that she never wanted to see him again because seeing him reminded her of what he'd done. Right after that he'd moved out. She wanted to tell him she was sorry for the hurtful, unforgiveable things she'd said. But when she opened her mouth to say the words, they wouldn't come out. There was a big gap between wanting to make peace for the sake of their son, and forgiving him for letting Joshua be stolen.

Marcie's eyes welled with tears again, but this time she was crying, not only for Joshua, but also for herself. She pulled away from Joe and lay down on the hard floor, turning her back on him and closing her eyes. She didn't sleep for a long time. Her brain swirled with all the things she'd never said to him. All the times she hadn't reached out to soothe his pain.

The last thing she remembered before falling asleep was that Joe was still sitting up, his back propped against the wall.

Chapter Twelve

The screeching and static of the walkie-talkie split the air, shocking Marcie awake. She shot upright, her heart hammering against her chest. Walkie-talkie. *Howard.*

She glanced around. Where was it? Then she remembered it was next to the heater, plugged into the same extension cord. As she threw off the blanket so she could crawl toward the walkie-talkie, she looked for Joe.

She didn't see him. "Joe?" she said softly, just as Howard's awful voice came through the walkie-talkie.

"Marcie! Time to rise and shine," Howard said on a rough laugh. "Hope it's not too early for you."

Joe appeared from out of the shadows on the other side of the cabin as she was picking up the walkie-talkie. He offered her a tin cup of water but she shook her head and held out the radio.

"Answer him but don't tell him anything. Just see what he wants," Joe whispered. "I've got an idea."

She frowned. Joe seemed different this morning from last night. Today he had an air of confidence that she hadn't seen before. "What? What's your idea?" she asked, then realized that she was whispering, too. Howard couldn't hear her unless she pressed the talk button on her device, but like Joe, she was still afraid to speak loudly, even if the button wasn't pushed.

Static sounded. "Marcie! Hey, woman, wake up! Don't you want your kid?"

Joe nodded at the radio.

She pressed the talk button. "I'm here," she said. "Where's my son? I want him *now!*" Releasing the button, she looked directly at Joe. "What idea? Tell me."

He shook his head. "You don't need to know that right now. Just listen to Howard."

"What? I don't need—?"

Howard's voice interrupted her. "Yeah, yeah. You're awfully demanding for somebody who's not controlling things. Hold your horses and listen to me."

"What do you mean I don't need to know?" she said shortly to Joe. "How am I supposed to—?"

"Hey! Are you listening?" Howard asked.

Glaring at Joe, she pushed the button just long enough to say, "Yes, Howard. I'm listening." Then to Joe, she said, "Now tell me what your idea is, so I'll know what I'm talking about."

"All you need to do is agree with whatever he says. Just do that, would you?" Joe said impatiently.

"In exactly twenty minutes," Howard continued, "I want you out of that house and down the stairs. Got it? So here's what you do. You bring the bag of money and nothing else down the stairs and out to the road."

"What's wrong with you?" Marcie asked Joe, who was frowning.

Joe nodded toward the walkie-talkie. "Talk to him."

She stood there, her thumb poised over the button, so furious at Joe her ears burned. "I don't know what to tell him, now do I?"

"Marcie, just answer him."

Just answer him, she mocked in her mind as she pressed the button. "Okay," she said into the speaker. "Down to the road. Nothing but the money."

"Dammit, woman!" Howard growled. "What are you doing over there? You'd better answer me when I talk to you or I can stop this right now and you'll never see your kid again."

"I was—I was getting the bag of money," she said, trying to sound afraid, although she figured it came across as more angry than scared.

"You've got twenty minutes to do that. Right now you pay attention to me."

"O-okay."

"Now you listen good. Bring the money and the walkie-talkie with you. Wait at the foot of the stairs until I call you and tell you what to do next."

Marcie pressed the button. "Howard? Why all this spy stuff? I'm here, right where you told me to be. I have the money with me. Just bring me my son!"

"Don't make me mad, Marcie. I'm getting tired of this. Have you forgotten what'll happen if you don't do exactly what I tell you?"

"No," she said quickly, Howard's threat to cut off Joshua's finger blossoming in her mind in full color. "No, no, I haven't. Okay. Twenty minutes. Bottom of the stairs. I swear, Howard, if you—"

Joe raised his hand. Marcie gave him a look that

should have dropped him where he stood, but she let go of the button. "What?"

"Watch what you say. And remember, he doesn't know I'm here. That's our ace in the hole."

She rolled her eyes. "Thanks. I couldn't possibly have figured that out by myself."

Howard started talking again. "And, woman? You better hope you've got enough money there, or you won't have your money or your kid."

"I want to talk to Joshua," she said.

Joe scowled and held up his hand.

She sliced her hand through the air in the universal gesture for *shut up*.

Increased static announced Howard opening his mic again. "Someone needs to teach you how to do what you're told." As he spoke, Marcie could hear something in the background. Something that sounded a lot like a child crying.

"Oh, I hear him. Please. Let me talk to my baby. I'll do anything you want."

"I swear, woman, the kid's gonna be the one that suffers if you don't stop yammering."

"I'm—I'm sorry. I'm just so afraid. How do I know I can trust you to bring my child to me?" She let go of the talk button.

"I told you not to say anything. Just to agree to what he says," Joe said.

"You haven't been here. I've begged him to let me talk to Joshua every single time he calls. I need to keep that up."

Howard's voice broke in. "Well, I reckon you're just

going to have to decide—do you want your kid back or not?"

Joe held her gaze for a few seconds, then nodded. "Do what you think is best."

Marcie wondered if he were being sarcastic, but his gaze was clear and earnest and his tone was respectful. "Thanks," she said.

Joe nodded his approval of what she was saying.

She pressed the talk button. "I want him back, Howard. I want him *now!*"

"I've had enough of you."

"Howard?" she said. "Howard! When are you coming?" She sniffed in frustration and released the button. "It sounds completely dead now. Do you think he turned the walkie-talkie off?"

"Maybe."

She stomped over to set the walkie-talkie in the charger. Then she confronted Joe with her hands propped on her hips. "What was all that? I have handled this alone up to now. Why couldn't you trust me?"

"I didn't want you to make him too angry. Like I said before, it's good, in fact it's essential to keep the upper hand, but it's a fine line—"

"Stop it!" she cried. "Just stop with the damn closing remarks. I hate it when you sound like a lawyer."

He raised his brows.

She drew a long breath. "Okay," she said, raising her hands, palm out, in a gesture of surrender. "Okay. I'm sorry. Can you tell me now what your big idea is? Now that there's no chance of me spilling it to Howard?"

"That's not why I didn't want to tell you."

"Then why?" she demanded.

"I'd wanted to talk to you before he called. I wanted to tell you what I was thinking, see if you thought it was a good idea, and I didn't want to be telling you while you were trying to talk to him."

"Oh." Joe's explanation made sense. The irritation and frustration burning inside her eased. "Okay," she said. "Tell me about it."

"I was hoping that Howard would want you out of the house for the exchange. Out in the open is much safer for him. You can't surprise him with a weapon or have an accomplice sneak up on him. That way he can control the swap."

"That makes sense—for him."

"Right. That's why you're going to refuse to come out of the house. Here's what we're going to do."

Marcie clutched the walkie-talkie to her chest as she stared out the window. Behind her Joe had his elbows on the counter and was scribbling something with a pen on the back of an envelope Marcie had found in her purse.

"What time is it?" Marcie asked.

"About three minutes later than the last time you asked," Joe muttered.

"Seriously. What time?" she insisted.

"Eight-thirty."

"It's been at least twenty-five minutes. Why doesn't he come on?" she said. "I'm going to be a nervous wreck by the time he gets here." She turned around and looked at Joe. She hadn't asked him what he wanted the pen and paper for. At first she'd thought he might be working out how he was going to overpower Howard, since his lawyer's brain worked better from an outline, no matter what he was planning. But he'd been writing too long and too consistently. "What are you writing?"

He didn't answer. The pen continued to scratch on the paper. Marcie didn't ask again. She had the sense that whatever he was writing was extremely important to him. She turned back to the window to watch for Howard's green pickup truck.

"A will," Joe said.

Her breath caught in her throat. "A w-will?" she stammered. "What do you think is going to happen?"

"Nothing, but I've never done a will. You'd think I of all people would have already taken care of that, but I guess even attorneys are subject to the arrogance of youth. Besides..." he began, then stopped.

Marcie filled in what he didn't say. People thought about wills when they had someone they wanted to make sure would be cared for. Joe had lost his son and his wife. So why would he make a will? Her eyes filled with tears for about the two hundredth time since she'd seen her baby in the backseat of Rhoda's Nissan. She'd have thought she would have been empty of tears and sadness by now. But apparently those wells were bottomless. Now Joe had hope again. Hope that he once again might have a wife and son to care for. And... he thought he might die before the day was over. Her heart wrenched so suddenly and tightly in her chest that she gasped.

"Marcie?" he said, glancing at her in concern.

"Joe, you're not thinking that Howard is capable of

killing, are you?" She heard the click of the ballpoint pen and the paper being folded.

"I think everybody is capable of killing."

"Don't philosophize, please. Just answer the question."

"I'm not philosophizing," he said. "I really do think everybody could kill if they had to. You'd kill for Joshua, wouldn't you?"

She nodded without hesitation. *And to save you.*

"There. See. And I certainly would. For Joshua or you."

Marcie realized that she believed him, and believing him gave her a depth of courage and determination that she'd never felt before. "What would Howard kill for, I wonder?"

"I think he'd kill for Rhoda. I believe he loves her. And I think that's what makes him dangerous. The fact that he'd do anything for her."

The implications of his words stabbed into her with the force of a knife. She realized that she'd never thought about Howard as a person. She'd never considered that he might love someone, or that he was doing this for any other reason than greed. But now that she thought about him in this new light, the implications were horrific. He would kill Joe and her if it meant that Rhoda could keep Joshua.

She turned to face Joe. In his gaze, she saw the answer to her next question. But she asked it anyway. "You think he'd kill to keep Rhoda from losing Joshua, don't you?"

He dropped his gaze as he nodded.

"That's why you don't want me to go out there."

"All he has to do is shoot you, then he's got the money and Rhoda's got the child she always wanted."

"Oh, my God," she said. "I didn't think about that at all." She turned back to the window. "Joe? You've told me what I'm supposed to do, but what about you? What are you planning to do once he comes inside?"

"Don't worry about that. Your biggest job is to forget that I'm even here. You *have* to stay focused on Howard. Don't even think about me. If you do, you might give me away."

"I can handle it, Joe. I know I can."

"Just remember. Everything we're doing is for Joshua." He held out the folded envelope. "Put this in your purse."

"Joe—you don't need this," she began, but the determination in his expression stopped her. She meekly tucked the envelope down into her bag. Just as she did, the walkie-talkie screeched. Marcie jumped and almost dropped it. As she was scrabbling to catch it, Howard's voice crackled through the static.

"Where the hell are you, woman? You're supposed to be down here in the middle of the road."

Marcie glanced at Joe and saw his slight nod, then pressed the talk button. "I'm here, Howard. In the house."

"Well get your butt down here like I told you. I've got the kid and I've got a sharp knife. If you ain't down here in the next ten seconds, I'll cut off a finger. I swear I will."

"Oh, no, you won't," Marcie growled. "If you touch

one hair on his head, I'll burn this money. I swear I will."

"You won't do that," Howard said. "That house'll go up like a box of matches, with you in it. Now get down here."

Joe watched his wife. He'd told her she needed to be totally focused on her job, which was to get Howard up the stairs and into the house. Well, she was focused all right. He was pretty sure if Howard were in the same room with her, she'd have his eyes clawed out inside of a minute.

She was like a mother lion, protecting her cub. Joe hadn't imagined how good she would be at her part of their plan. As for his role, he had no idea if it would work. He just had to react to what Howard did. He hoped he could manage to keep Howard busy long enough to allow Marcie to run to the pickup. He hadn't told her what she'd have to do yet because he wanted her full of adrenaline and ready for anything. Then when he yelled at her to make a run for it, he was counting on her reacting on instinct rather than stopping to think about what she was doing.

"I've tested some of the money to see if it burns fast. It does, Howard. It does."

Through the walkie-talkie, Howard cursed.

"I'm not coming down there. You come up here. *And you bring my son.* Do you understand?"

The other end of the walkie-talkie stayed silent, so Marcie pushed the talk button again. "Howard? I want to talk to him. Hold the walkie-talkie so he can talk into it. I want to hear him now!"

After a pause, she heard the mic click on. "You bitch. You can't order me around. I'll shoot the house down. I've got my rifle."

Joe put his hand on Marcie's arm, but she shrugged it off. "My child, Howard. I want to hear my child talk. Otherwise you go ahead and shoot. I'll be burning money."

"All right, all right. Hang on," Howard said, then cut off his mic for another few moments. "I can't let him talk to you. He's tied up and got duct tape on his mouth."

"Take it off!"

"Nope." The static stopped.

Marcie frowned at her walkie-talkie. "What's he—?"

Then amidst static, Howard said, "Nope. I can't—I can't watch him and you at the same time."

"Do it now! Take that tape off his mouth now. He's probably scared to death!"

As Joe listened to the two of them he came to a stunning realization. It surprised him that he hadn't thought about it before. Howard didn't have Joshua. He'd driven to the house in his pickup, maybe with a rifle, maybe not. But he'd come here expecting Marcie to be waiting in the middle of the road with a sack of money. He'd tell her to leave the money in the middle of the road and go back to the house. She'd demand to see her child, but Howard would tell her that the only way she'd get Joshua back was to obey him. Then, when she'd done what he'd told her to, he'd pick up the money and speed away, back to Rhoda and Joshua, and the three of them would be miles and miles from Louisiana by nightfall. Joe nodded to himself in satisfaction. Knowing that

Joshua wasn't in the pickup made his plan a lot easier. He touched Marcie on the arm.

"What?" she asked shortly. "You told me to focus. I'm focused. Don't interrupt."

"What you said about the money—that's really smart. Tell him to bring Joshua up here now or you'll start lighting bills on fire and dropping them over the rail."

"Now you want me out there? I thought you didn't want me to get shot."

"All you have to do is go to the railing and drop the burning bills over the edge. You'll be shielded somewhat by the corner of the house."

Marcie gazed at him with narrowed eyes. "Okay. I'll try it. All we're doing now is arguing back and forth." She pressed the talk button. "Howard, bring Joshua up here right now. I've got your money, but I'm not coming down there. I don't trust you for one second."

"I'll shoot the stilts and that house'll fall flat with you in it. I'm telling you for the last time. Get down here with that money!"

"Oh, I'll send your money down," she said mockingly. "One bill at a time. Watch for it. You can't miss it." She let go of the talk button and set the walkie-talkie down.

"Take the walkie-talkie with you," Joe said.

"I'm going to need both hands to light the bills on fire and throw them over the rail. I'll just yell at him."

"You've got to stay in the shadow of the house, as close to the door as you can."

She picked up a stack of hundreds from the bag, tore

the wrapper off, then peeled off about a dozen. "Have you seen any matches?" she asked.

Joe searched for a moment. "Here's a candle lighter in the drawer, if it works." He clicked it and a small yellow flame sprang up from its tip.

"Drawer?" Marcie said. "There's a drawer?"

Joe nodded. "Two of them. They're pretty shallow, though."

"I didn't see them," she said, reaching for the lighter, but Joe held on to it.

"Marcie, remember. Stay close to the door. If you see him raise his rifle, duck back inside."

She nodded and opened the door.

"Wait!" Joe whispered. "I'm putting the walkie-talkie right here on the floor next to the door." His pulse began to race as she stepped out onto the stoop. He was dying to look out and see if he could see Howard's pickup, but he didn't dare. Everything, even their lives, depended on Howard not knowing he was there.

"Here you go, Howard," Marcie called. "In case you can't see them from there, these are hundreds. Benjamins."

The walkie-talkie crackled. "…burning that money… regret it." Joe couldn't hear everything Howard said, but he got the gist of it.

"Where is he?" he asked.

"Still in the truck," she answered. Then she yelled, "Two hundred at a time, Howard!"

"Be careful," Joe warned her. "If he opens the door and starts to get out, he could be going for his rifle."

"I'm watching him," she said as Howard's voice interrupted her.

"Okay, okay. You win! I'm bringing the kid up."

"Now it's three hundred at a time!" she shouted.

The walkie-talkie crackled again. "Stop it! I'm coming up."

"Good job," Joe said. "Now get inside."

"No, wait. I want to see Joshua."

"Marcie!"

"I am not moving until I can see my baby." She heard Joe muttering curses but her attention was on Howard. He got out of the pickup, then opened the rear door and leaned inside. She held her breath as she waited for him to lift her little boy out of the rear seat.

"Joe, he's doing it. He's getting Joshua. Look through the window. He won't be able to see a tiny space in the curtains. Look, Joe."

The curtains fluttered as Joe parted them slightly. "What do you see?" he asked her.

"Nothing yet. He's doing something—maybe unhooking the child seat. Wait. He's straightening up."

The walkie-talkie crackled with Howard's yell. "Marcie!"

"I'm here." She waved.

"Careful," Joe whispered.

"Get inside," Howard demanded. "Or I'm not coming up."

"What?" she called out. "Howard, please. He's my baby."

"Because I said so." Howard's voice nearly drowned out Joe's. "Get inside and wait there. I'm coming up the stairs with the kid, but I swear I'll drop him right back down them. Now get in there and stay there. You got me?"

"What's he doing?" she asked Joe.

"I don't know," Joe said. "Maybe he's afraid you have a weapon."

She clicked the talk button. "Okay, okay. But you'd better not hurt my baby."

When Marcie closed the door, Joe was still at the window, watching Howard. "He's pulling something out of the backseat," he said.

She went over to the window. Joe held out his arm and made room for her to stand in front of him. That way both of them could look out through the same tiny crack in the curtains. "See him?" Joe asked.

"Oh, yes," Marcie breathed. "Look. He's got him. Oh, no, he's got Joshua wrapped in a blanket. Do you think he's all right? You don't think he's sick, do you?"

Joe saw the same thing Marcie did, but he immediately drew a different conclusion. Howard was lifting a bundle into his arms, holding it as if he were holding a sleeping child, but Joe knew better. Howard didn't have Joshua.

Chapter Thirteen

Joe sighed in frustration and a bit of relief. Howard didn't have Joshua. He'd been right about the guy. He really did love Rhoda too much to take the child away from her, or maybe she wouldn't let him. Joe craved a glimpse of his son, but he was glad that he didn't have to worry about making sure his child was all right while trying to take Howard down.

Whatever Howard's reason, his plan all along had been to overpower Marcie, then take the money and run. Rhoda was probably waiting with Joshua for Howard to pick them up. The three of them would be out of the state and headed for parts unknown hours before Marcie could find help on this bayou road.

But Howard hadn't counted on Joe being there. And Joe was counting on that. He intended for this day to end with Howard and Rhoda in custody for kidnapping, and his son back in his wife's arms.

"Oh," Marcie said, pressing her hand to her throat. "I feel faint. I'd almost given up ever seeing him again. He's here, Joe." Her voice sounded choked. "I had no idea how I would react if I ever got the chance to see my baby again, to hold him, to have him come home with us." She wrapped her other arm around Joe's waist and hugged him. "I don't think I've ever been this happy in my entire life."

Her lilting tone and happy words ripped through Joe's heart like a knife through rotten cloth, leaving ugly jagged edges. How was he going to tell her? He was afraid that she'd break down completely, and he needed her to be strong, because without her, Joe's plan would fail. He swallowed. "Listen to me, hon," Joe said. "Don't let your emotions overwhelm you. We've still got to overpower Howard and restrain him, remember?"

He felt her head move as she nodded. "I know. I know. And we've got to do it without hurting or endangering Joshua. I can do it, Joe. I'm ready."

"Okay," he said. "Then we've got to get away from the window and get set up."

"I want to watch for a little while longer. Just until he—"

"Marcie, listen." Joe took her arm from around his waist and stepped away from her. "We've got to be ready. We can't make even one mistake. If we do, we may lose—everything." Joe gritted his teeth. He hated what he was doing. He was in effect lying to her. He had to pretend that he believed it was Joshua in that bundle. Otherwise Marcie would know something was wrong. If he slipped up and gave her any hint that Howard didn't have Joshua, at best he could ruin everything. At worst, he could get them both hurt or killed.

She stepped away from the window and squared her

shoulders. "Okay. You want me here, right beside the door?"

"Yes. There. When he pushes or kicks the door open, you'll be arm's length from him. I'll be behind the door." He gestured vaguely in that direction. He hadn't told her much about what he was planning to do. "Now, do you have the spray?"

She nodded. "What are you going to use as a weapon?" she asked.

"Shh." He held his finger to his mouth as heavy footsteps sounded on the pier. Howard was almost here, and just in time to save Joe from answering. He'd inventoried and assessed everything he could find in the house, everything in Marcie's purse and everything in their car. Marcie would use her pepper spray to initially disable Howard, but stinging eyes was not enough of a deterrent. He needed something that would render Howard unconscious or at least incapable of fighting back.

The weapon he'd settled on was unconventional at best, but it was probably the one that could do the most damage in the shortest amount of time, and last long enough for Joe to tie him up. But he couldn't allow Marcie to even catch a glimpse of what he'd chosen. She wouldn't let him within a hundred yards of Joshua if she knew what he was planning to use.

Marcie stood right next to the closed door, the can of pepper spray at the ready in her right hand and several bungee cords tucked into the waistband of her jeans. She was so nervous that her hands wouldn't stop shaking, and she had to clamp her jaw to stop her teeth from chattering. She was dying to see what Joe was doing, but he had insisted on keeping the curtains closed, which put them in near total darkness. He wanted to catch Howard off guard when he stepped into the dark house. Also, Joe had commanded her not to take her eyes off the door.

"You've got to focus on nothing but making sure the pepper spray goes directly into his eyes," he told her. "He's probably going to be talking, maybe even threatening you. But you can't listen to him, because if you miss, then it won't matter what I've planned to do, because if he's not hurting and if he doesn't let go of the blanket, I can't take him down. It won't matter that he doesn't know I'm here. At full strength, he's a lot stronger than me."

She could hear the rustling of his clothing and an occasional metallic click as he worked on whatever he was doing. Then the generator kicked on and drowned out his quiet movements.

At that moment, Howard's boots clomped up the stairs to the house. Marcie thought his footsteps sounded unusually heavy, even for a man of his size. Her heart leapt. That had to be because he was carrying Joshua. She heard him grunt with effort as he reached the top step and set his boot onto the stoop. The floor shuddered. Marcie swallowed, drew in a fortifying breath and raised the can of spray. She placed her finger on the nozzle and concentrated on the door.

With a grunt louder than his first one, Howard kicked the door with his boot. The noise echoed off the walls. Marcie tensed.

"I'm coming in, Marcie," he said loudly. "I've got the

kid. You stand away from the door. Try anything and I'll turn around and throw him over the rail. Got that? I'll throw. Him. Over."

"Yes," she said, not having to fake the quaver in her voice. She gritted her teeth and tried not to think about Joshua or about what Joe was doing. She had to concentrate. She only had one chance to do this right.

She watched the doorknob as Howard turned it and the door began to ease open. As the door swung open, Marcie's heart screamed at her to look at the bundle in his arms. Just one glimpse wouldn't hurt, would it?

Focus. She fought her mother's instinct to care for her child and it was the hardest thing she'd ever had to do in her life.

Focus! Her entire world seemed to be moving in slow motion, including her own movements. Raising her arm, she fixed her gaze on his head, which was turning in her direction. When she saw the side of his face as he turned his head toward her, she pressed the nozzle, aiming it directly at his eyes. The sound of the aerosol was muffled by Howard's agonized roar. He threw up an arm to ward off the spray and when he did the bundle dropped to the floor. Then he lunged at her. She dove beneath his arm toward the bundle, screaming, "Joshua!" over and over. Somewhere along the way she dropped the spray can.

Joe timed his movement to the sound of the aerosol spray. He propelled himself at Howard at the same instant that Howard lunged at Marcie. Joe had no idea how much—if any—spray had gone into Howard's eyes. But some had, judging by the man's bellows.

Clutching the fiery hot space heater by the handle on the top, he held it in front of him like a shield as he propelled himself forward. He'd cushioned the uninsulated back with a torn piece of the ratty blanket, but as he landed on top of the bigger man with the heater between them, the metal seared his hands and chest.

Howard screamed like a woman as Joe growled out loud and pressed the coils into the back of Howard's head with all the strength he had. He knew he had only a split second to inflict as much damage as possible, and he'd underestimated the pain of the burning metal against his own skin, even through the blanket. But the longer he could hold on, the better chance he'd have of disabling Howard. The smell of burning hair filled the air as Howard flailed and bucked. Joe bore down on him with all his might. He felt a tug against his hands, as the electrical cord stretched to its limit. Then the tug suddenly relaxed and he knew the heater had come unplugged.

"Marcie!" he yelled. "Bungee cords—now! *Come on, Marcie!*" He registered her sobs in the part of his brain that was always aware of her, so he knew she'd found out that the bundle of blankets was not her child.

Joe felt himself being drawn to her, but he tamped down that urge with all his will. If he let her grief and shock distract him, he might lose this fight. He'd known she'd be upset. He'd planned around it, but damn it he needed those cords. Grimacing with pain and effort, he leaned every bit of his weight on the still blazing hot heater.

"Marcie!" he yelled again as Howard tried to buck

him off. He had to get ready to tie up Howard. He only
hoped Howard was hurting enough that he wouldn't
be able to throw him off. Joe rose up, still pressing the
coils against Howard's cheek, and grabbed the man's
left hand. With an effort, he swung his left knee forward and pinned the hand. Then he finally let go of the
heater and drew his right knee forward to pin Howard's
right hand. The heater tumbled onto the floor.

Howard lifted his head, roaring like a wounded lion.
His neck and the side of his face bore a red-and-black
pattern of the exposed heater coils. It was an ugly sight.
Joe swallowed hard and looked at the man's hands. He
took a breath to yell for Marcie one last time, but, mi-
raculously, she was there with the cords.

Resisting the urge to double his fist and coldcock
Howard on the side of the head, Joe instead grabbed a
bungee cord and slipped one end like a lasso over Howard's left wrist. Then, with a twist, he yanked Howard's
right wrist up and wrapped the elastic cord back and
forth around both wrists. As he worked, heaving with
the effort and doing his best to ignore the pain in his
burned hands, Howard's hefty body gave up the fight
and collapsed. He lay limp. His roar deflated into a low
moaning. His entire torso trembled. Probably shock
from the pain. After a few seconds of struggle, Joe finally managed to hook the bungee cord tightly onto
itself.

Only then did he dare to get off the man and stand
up. His head spun dizzily and he had trouble catching
his breath. For a few seconds he bent at the waist and

propped his hands on his knees like a basketball player, easing the pressure on his lungs.

"Marcie, can you…wrap his ankles?" he gasped. "If he kicks, stop. I'll…get it."

He hadn't realized how tense he'd been. Or how focused. But obviously his body had pumped massive quantities of adrenaline to his muscles and nerves, because now that he'd stopped, his limbs tingled and trembled with the aftereffects. It took a few seconds for him to be able to breathe normally.

When he finally straightened, his palms felt lit on fire. He turned them up and saw that they were bright red and he could see blisters beginning to form. That was going to be a problem very soon, so he needed to make sure Howard was sufficiently trussed now.

Howard was still moaning when Joe checked Marcie's work with the bungee cord on Howard's ankles. She'd done a good job. He felt the tension in both cords and adjusted Marcie's a little and his own a lot. He'd wound the elastic way too tight in his haste to put Howard out of commission.

As soon as he was sure the cords were tight enough to keep Howard from getting loose, but not so tight that they cut off his circulation, he turned to Marcie.

Behind him, Howard was beginning to stir. "You burned me," he muttered. "I'll sue."

Marcie was crouched on the floor, holding two more bungee cords. When she raised her gaze to his, her face looked haunted and her normally lovely, sparkly eyes were dull.

"He didn't bring Joshua," she said flatly. "But you

knew that he wouldn't, didn't you? It was your plan all along, wasn't it? You knew he didn't have my baby."

Joe held out a hand to help her to her feet, but she ignored it and rose on her own. She tossed the cords onto the floor and stood there, staring at Howard, who had quit struggling so much, but was still moaning and muttering an occasional curse, presumably aimed at them. "You wouldn't have used the heater if you'd thought he'd be holding Joshua."

"Marcie, hon, come here."

She ignored that, too.

"I'm sure Joshua is with Rhoda," he said. "Howard wanted the money. But Rhoda loves Joshua. You know that. You said it yourself. So she wasn't about to risk Howard doing something to him, either accidentally or on purpose."

She nodded, then looked up at him. "She's going to run," she said. "I'll never see my baby again."

Joe held out his arms, but Marcie shrank away from him and wrapped her arms around herself. "Hon," he said. "We don't know that she's running. She and Joshua are probably back at her house."

But Marcie was shaking her head. "No. No. No. She wouldn't sit there and wait for the police. I don't even think she'd wait for Howard. If he did this once he'd do it again. She's taken my baby and run—some place where we'll never find them."

"You can't know that," he protested.

Marcie straightened and fixed him with a gaze. "Oh, yes, I can."

"But how? Why are you so sure?" he asked, bewildered.

"Because it's what I would do."

Joe stared at Marcie. Of course. As soon as she'd said those words—words only a mother could say with confidence—he knew that was what was happening. If Rhoda hadn't already taken Joshua and left, she was probably preparing to go right now.

Joe stalked over to where Howard was lying on his stomach, with his hands tied behind his back. He was moaning and cursing. Joe nudged him in the side with the toe of his shoe.

"Ahh, you son of a bitch, you burned me. Need a doctor," Howard gasped.

"Where's Rhoda?" he asked him.

"Go to hell," Howard muttered.

"Where is she, Howard? I can burn the other side of your face, you know."

"Went back to the house."

Joe turned back to Marcie. "Come on, Marcie. Let's go. We need to get to Rhoda's house. She's probably waiting there for Howard to pick them up. We need to get there before she decides Howard isn't coming and takes off on her own."

"But the car's stuck." Then, for the first time since Howard came into the house, Marcie perked up. She went to the door and looked outside. "Howard's truck! We can take his truck and then if Rhoda does see us, she'll think it's Howard."

"That's right, hon." Joe crouched down beside Howard and shook his shoulder. "Howard. Where are your keys?"

"Need doctor," Howard whispered. "Hurting bad."

"Come on, Howard. Do I need to pat you down? I'll do it."

The only sound from Howard was a long groan.

Joe patted Howard's pockets and came up with a set of keys. "Here we go," he said, holding up the keys. "Marcie, think you can drive?"

"I guess so, if I have to. Why?"

Joe held out his hands, which were about half-covered in clear blisters now. She looked at them, made a small, low sound in distress, then took the keys. "Are we ready to go?" she asked.

"Yeah," he replied. "We can come back and get this stuff later. Our first priority is to find Rhoda and call the police."

Marcie drove the pickup. Despite its creakiness and filth, the engine was surprisingly peppy. The starter groaned, as did the transmission when she shifted gears, but she didn't have any trouble driving it. She didn't speak on the drive and neither did Joe. Her head was filled with worry about Joshua and anger at Joe for not warning her that Howard didn't have her baby.

But then, a question wormed its way into her consciousness. If she'd known Joshua wasn't there, could she have been as convincing as a mother desperate to see and hold her child? She pushed away the argument that Joe had done the best thing for the situation. She wanted to wallow in her grief and anger a little while longer.

As they approached Rhoda's house, Marcie said shortly, "I was about here when Howard called me yesterday."

Joe looked at his phone. "I've got two bars," he said. He dialed the number Ethan Delancey had given him.

"Detective Delancey?" he asked when someone answered.

"Joe Powers," Ethan said on an audible sigh. "I'm glad to hear from you. Are you and your wife all right?"

"Yeah, we're fine." There was a lot unsaid in that terse comment, and Joe knew that eventually both he and Marcie would have to go through it all in excruciating detail, but for now— "Fine," he repeated. "We're in Howard's truck, almost to Rhoda's house."

"I know you don't have your son," Ethan said without preamble. "I've been trying to call you, but your phone kept going to voice mail."

"That's right. There's no cell service in the middle of Bayou DeChez," Joe said wryly. "We're hoping Rhoda's at her house with Joshua."

"I ordered surveillance on Rhoda Sumner's house yesterday morning, as soon as I left your house. There was no activity at all at the house until this morning, when one of my officers reported that she and a toddler were brought to the house in an old green pickup that I'm assuming is Howard Lelievre's. Just about twenty minutes ago, she put two suitcases in her car, then she and the toddler got into the car and headed north on I-55. My officer stopped her and took her into custody."

Joe breathed a sigh of relief. "That's great. Where are they now?"

"They're at the Hammond Police Department, right off I-55. You know how to get there?"

"Thomas Street, right? I can get there. Who should we ask for?"

"I tell you what. I'll be at the front desk. If something comes up and I'm not there, call me on my cell."

"Detective," Joe said, "thank you for stopping Rhoda. I can't tell you how grateful we are. We'll be there in about twenty minutes." He started to wipe a hand across his face, then saw the tissues wrapped around his palms. "I know where Howard is. He's in a stilt house on Bayou DeChez, a few miles west of Rhoda's house. He's tied up with bungee cords and his face and neck and upper back have been burned. He's the kidnapper who was demanding a ransom for Joshua. I'm sure the police are going to have a lot of questions for me. Please tell them I'm available anytime. I'm willing to do whatever I need to. I'm the one who burned him and left him there, tied up."

"I see," Ethan said. "I'll call the Killian P.D. and have them get somebody out there. They'll be calling you for a statement."

"Thanks, Detective."

"How's your wife?"

Joe glanced at Marcie, who hadn't taken her eyes off the road. Her hands were white-knuckled on the steering wheel. "We're both hanging in there, I guess."

"I need to let you know that the police chief in Hammond has ordered that the Department of Protective Child Services be brought in to take care of the boy."

"What? Why?" Joe blurted before he was able to control himself.

Marcie glanced over at him, disturbed by his tone. "What is it?" she asked.

"I'm sure you know why. You must have had experience with this type of situation at your job. Your son was nine months old when he was taken. He's thirty-three months old now. Obviously he's not going to remember you."

This time Joe was successful at controlling his outburst. He swallowed the anguished protest he wanted to make. "I don't think I agree with that," he said carefully.

Marcie sent him a sidelong glance. "Joe!" she said. "What's wrong?"

He just shook his head.

"I'm sorry. I wanted to give you a heads-up so you could prepare Marcie." Ethan sighed.

"Yeah," Joe said wryly. "Thanks."

"What's the matter?" Marcie said as soon as he hung up. "What did he say?"

Joe pocketed the phone, trying to figure out if there was any way to tell her about Child Services without sending her over the edge. He could feel her brittle control and he knew from past experience just how fragile that control was.

Chapter Fourteen

"Joe? What did Detective Delancey say? Is it something about Joshua?" Marcie asked, tugging at Joe's arm.

Joe grimaced. "Why don't we get some coffee? There's a diner in Killian and we're almost there. Maybe even some breakfast?"

"No! I don't want anything except my baby. What. Did. He. Tell. You?"

Joe saw Marcie's fingers tighten even more on the steering wheel. "They did find Rhoda," he said, choosing his words very carefully, "and she had Joshua with her."

Marcie threw her head back. "Ahh." She sighed. "Thank God. He's all right? He's good?"

"Apparently he's fine. They've taken them to Hammond, to the police station."

"We have to go. We have to get there now! How far is it to Hammond?"

"Marcie," Joe said, laying his hand lightly on her arm. "Pull over. You're nervous as a cat and you shouldn't be driving."

"No, Joe. That'll just waste time. We've got to get there. It's our son. My baby!"

"Pull over!" Joe shouted. "Now!"

Marcie jumped and shot him an alarmed look, but she stopped the truck and folded her arms. "Okay, Joe," she said, biting off each word. "I've stopped. What are you going to do? You can't drive. Your palms are covered with blisters. I don't know why you're being so mean. I'm perfectly capable of driving. I'm fine. I'm—" Her voice cracked.

Tears formed in her eyes and slipped down her cheeks. Joe wanted to apologize to her for yelling. He'd never raised his voice to her. Never needed to. But right now he was just as anxious as she was to see Joshua. He wanted to hold him, to kiss and hug his son. He wanted to be able to hand Marcie their child, to see her face when she got to hold her little boy for the first time in almost two years. And he knew that's what Marcie wanted, too.

But he knew it was going to be a long, painful time before either one of them could touch their child, or kiss him or hold him. It was going to be a long time—if ever—before the three of them were a family again.

What kind of coward was he that he couldn't tell her what Detective Delancey had told him? He couldn't bear to be the one to tell her that she couldn't talk to or touch her child. He was that much of a coward.

"Change seats," he growled, opening the passenger door. His hand burned and he felt blisters pop. "I'm going to drive."

"This ought to be good," she snapped. "Look at you.

Your hands are covered with blisters. How do you think you're going to drive?"

"Pretty damn carefully," he stormed at her.

With a sniff of frustration, she put the pickup in Neutral and engaged the emergency brake. Climbing out of the driver's seat, she walked around the front of the pickup as Joe walked around the back and got behind the wheel. He carefully released the brake, then shifted into first. He gritted his teeth as more blisters popped on his palms.

It took about twenty minutes to get to the Hammond Police Department. By the time they were parked, Marcie had handed Joe about a dozen tissues to wrap his hands in. He parked the truck and stepped on the emergency brake, and for a moment, he just sat, staring at his tissue-wrapped hands on the steering wheel.

"Joe?"

He clenched his teeth, took a long breath, then turned to Marcie. "I have to tell you something before we go in there."

She turned pale. "No, Joe. You said he was all right."

"He is all right, hon. Just listen to me. You need to know that...there are procedures for this kind of thing."

"No, Joe. No procedures. I need my baby. I need to hold him."

Joe swallowed hard. "I know, hon. I understand. But like I said, there are procedures for dealing with a child who's been stolen from his parents. Joshua was so young, and he's been gone for a long time."

"No," Marcie whispered brokenly. "No, Joe, please."

Her eyes were red, her cheeks chapped from the tears and the rain and the cool air. "Please. I need my baby."

Joe's heart ripped in two as he spoke the next few words. "Child Services is going to take him."

"No!" Marcie cried. "I won't let them. Child Services can't take my baby." She fumbled for the door latch and threw herself out of the truck. As soon as her feet hit the ground she was running toward the big front door of the station.

Joe jumped out and ran after her. He caught up with her about three steps from the door. He caught her arm and turned her around to face him. "Marcie, don't. You've got to handle this rationally. You have *got* to calm down. If you act irrationally, the Child Services people will wonder if you're capable of taking care of Joshua. You know they'll have access to the police's records of complaints against you for those previous incidents."

"Capable of taking—?" She choked and had to cough. "I am his *mother*. There is no one more capable."

"Hon, I know that," he said, feeling tears sting his own eyes. "But we have to convince them."

"Why, Joe?" The question sounded as if it were ripped from her throat. "Why would they keep him from me?" She almost collapsed in his arms. *Almost*.

But from somewhere, she drew on a reservoir of strength that he didn't realize she had left in her. She drew herself up to her full height, wiped her eyes, then pinned him with a glare.

"This is your fault," she whispered. "All of it. I have

been through hell these past two years, and so has my child. I would be happy if I never had to see you again."

Joe's eyes stung. "Marcie, come on. You're upset."

"You're damned right I'm upset. But I need to appear calm and collected. I'm going in there and I'm going to make sure those people know that I can take care of my child. You can go in there with me if you want, but—" She lifted a finger and pointed it at him. "Do not talk. Do not contradict me. Do not touch my child. I will do this on my own. Joshua and I don't need you." The whole time she talked, tears streamed down her face. She pulled a tissue from her purse and dried them, then straightened her back and walked into the station as if she were the police chief.

Joe wiped his wet cheeks with the cuff of his shirt. She was right. It all was his fault. All she'd ever done was try to deal with the devastation and grief he'd caused. For one ridiculous moment, he considered leaving the station. But he knew, even if she didn't, that both of them were in for hours and hours of questions, explanations and interrogations. He had to be here. Besides, he wasn't sure he'd be able to draw breath if they didn't allow him a glimpse of his son—and soon.

MARCIE STOPPED AT the door to the Hammond Police Department. She blotted the last of the tears from her cheeks, smoothed back her hair, then pushed the door open and stepped into the air-conditioned station.

Standing at the desk was the detective who'd come to see Joe the other day. Her brain registered again how much he and Joe looked alike, as he held out his hand to her.

"Mrs. Powers," he said. "I'm so glad to see you. Are you injured at all? We can have emergency medical technicians here within a few minutes."

She shook her head.

"What about some coffee or a glass of water?"

She shook her head again. "I'm ready to see my child," she said evenly.

Detective Delancey looked toward the door. "Where's your husband?"

She shrugged as the door pushed inward and Joe came in. Marcie tried not to look at him, but she couldn't help it. She hadn't really taken in his appearance once Howard was immobilized. In the sunlight that poured in through the glass doors, she saw that his hair was full of dust and dirt, his shirt was wrinkled and stained and his hands dripped with ragged facial tissues that were dotted with blood.

"Joe!" Delancey said. "What happened to your hands?"

"They're burned," Joe said, looking at them as if they didn't belong to him. "I guess I need to clean them up and bandage them."

Ethan was already turning to the desk sergeant. "Call for an EMT to treat—" He looked at Joe with a questioning glance.

"Blisters," Joe said ruefully.

"Second-degree burns on hands and forearms." Delancey turned to Joe again. "Anywhere else?"

Joe shook his head.

Marcie allowed herself to be irritated and impatient with the detective, who seemed far more concerned about Joe's burned hands than he did about her child. She caught his sleeve. "I want to see my baby now!" she said. "Where is he?"

Detective Delancey sent her an odd look. He glanced sidelong at Joe then back at her. "I'm sorry, Mrs. Powers, but the child is being questioned by a representative from the Department of Children and Family Services right now."

"You're sorry? You're *sorry?*" she said loudly. "That is *my* child in there—" she gestured vaguely "—and I want to see him right this minute. I have not seen him in two years. That is twenty-four months, sir."

A female police officer stepped up. Marcie didn't know where the woman had come from but she looked grim and determined, with one hand in her pocket and the other hand reaching for Marcie's arm. Marcie glared at her.

"Ma'am, why don't you come with me and we'll get a cup of coffee," the officer said, pausing just shy of touching Marcie's arm.

"I don't *want* a cup of coffee," Marcie snapped. "I want my child."

"Marcie, hon, they're going to help you," Joe said, stepping close to her and bending his head to speak quietly. "But first they have to follow the law. Everything's going to be fine, if you'll just—"

"Everything is *not* going to be fine. Just leave me alone," she said, her voice breaking. "Go get your hands fixed."

At that moment an EMT came through the glass doors with a medical kit in his hand. He stopped when he saw Joe. "Hi there," he said. "You must be my patient."

"Ethan," Joe said to the detective. "I really don't want to leave her."

Marcie sniffed. "Leave me, please," she said archly. Deep inside her she knew she was being irrational and mean, but she was afraid if she didn't hold on to this tremendous anger she felt toward Joe right now, she'd break down and start sobbing. She wasn't sure which would be worse in the critical eyes of Child Services as they ruled whether she could take care of her child. *Her child.* And right now she didn't care. She was doing the only thing she could do to stay in control. Anger was all she had right now.

As Joe went off with the EMT to get his hands treated, Detective Delancey laid a hand on Marcie's arm. She flinched, but quelled her initial urge to pull away. That would probably be resisting arrest, she thought with a wry, inward chuckle.

Delancey looked at her oddly for an instant, then composed his face. "Mrs. Powers, if you'll go with Officer Hatcher, I'll check with the official from Child Services and see what we can do about letting you see your son."

Suddenly, she was at a loss for words. She couldn't speak, could barely think. Had he really said she could see her son? Or she might be able to see her son? Momentarily confused, she allowed the officer to guide her to a kitchen and pour her a cup of coffee.

"It's fairly fresh," the officer said kindly.

Marcie burst into tears.

Chapter Fourteen

Joe walked up to the house that he and Marcie had bought together when they'd found out they were pregnant. He stood there looking at the doorbell as the past two weeks slid through his head.

Joshua had gone home with Marcie two days after Rhoda was arrested trying to leave the state with him. And Joe had gone back to his apartment. The psychologist assigned to them by Child Services had quickly seen that Joshua would be better off with Marcie than with a foster family.

The three of them were attending twice-weekly counseling sessions. In addition, a social worker visited the house once a week to ensure a smooth transition for Joshua back into his mother's life.

Joe was here this evening because Marcie had called and invited him to spend the evening with her and Joshua. From her nervous and slightly scattered phone call, he figured the invitation was an assignment from the psychologist or the social worker. But that was okay. That day in the police station, when his wife refused his help or comfort, it was painfully obvious that the two of them would never get back together. So when it came to his son, he would take anything he could get. Even an awkward, therapist-assigned evening with his estranged wife.

He rang the doorbell and took a long, calming breath as he waited for her to answer. From somewhere inside the house, he heard a sound that made him smile. It was Marcie, laughing. He peered through the sidelight at the foyer. After a couple of seconds, he saw her. She had on a sleeveless dress that drifted around her legs and she was barefoot. She came skipping through the foyer with a beautiful smile on her face, and quickly unlocked the door.

"Hi," she said brightly. "I didn't realize it was locked. Sorry." She beamed at him, then turned around and headed back the way she'd come. "We're in the kitchen," she called over her shoulder.

He followed, watching the hem of her dress float around her calves. It seemed to him that she left all the scents and freshness of spring in her wake. It made his heart ache to see her so happy. It hadn't been that long ago that he'd been convinced that neither one of them would ever smile again.

When he got to the kitchen, Joshua was sitting at the little table Marcie had bought for him, trying to fit plastic cubes and balls and pyramids into the same shaped holes of a brightly colored toy.

"Joshua, look. It's Daddy," Marcie said.

The toddler held up a ball. "Daddeee!" he cried, then dropped the ball into the round hole. "I'n a good boy!"

Joe crouched down beside him and brushed his hand

over his silky hair that was just like Marcie's. "You're a smart boy. Look what you did."

Joshua picked up the cube. "I'n a smar' boy," he repeated, then tried to push the cube into the triangular hole. When it wouldn't go, he banged it down a couple of times and started whimpering.

"Oh," Marcie muttered and started for him, but Joe held up a hand.

"I've got it," he said, "if that's okay."

"It's great," she replied. "I've still got to feed him. He's sleepy. That's why he's cranky."

Joe took the cube from Joshua's fingers.

"No!" Joshua snapped. "Mine."

"Hey, buddy, I know it's yours, but you don't bang it."

"Bang it. Bang it."

"Here." Joe gave the cube back to Joshua. "Let's put it right here." He pointed to the square hole.

"No," Joshua said, banging the cube against the triangular hole again.

Joe wrapped his hand around Joshua's tiny one. "No banging it. Okay?"

Joshua looked at Marcie, then back at Joe. "No bang it?"

"No bang it," Joe said, trying not to laugh. Behind him, Marcie's sweet laugh rang out like a bell.

"He didn't get a nap today because the social worker came by right when I was getting him into his crib," she said.

Joe guided Joshua's hand to the square hole. The cube dropped right in. "Yay," Joe said.

Joshua clapped his hands together and looked at Marcie. "Mama, look! I'n a good—I'n a smar' boy."

"Yes, you are," she said, sidling past Joe to bend down and plant a kiss on Joshua's cheek. "Mmm. You're a sweet boy, too."

"Swee' boy," he repeated.

Joe couldn't stop the stinging behind his eyelids any more than he could wipe away the grin that spread across his face. Marcie's gaze met his over Joshua's head and her eyes sparkled like they had when they were first married, and while she was pregnant, and every day after Joshua was born until—

"Joe?" Marcie interrupted his thoughts. "Would you mind feeding him while I finish getting dinner ready?"

"Sure. I'll feed him." He was amazed and delighted by his son. He hadn't gotten to spend much time with him at all. Several new cases had recently come into the NCMEC, so that by the time he'd gotten to the house on the few occasions when Marcie had invited him, Joshua had already been in bed or was just about to go. "What does he eat these days?"

"Anything he can get his hands on. Here," she said, handing Joe a bowl with cut-up pasta and cream sauce. "And here's his spoon. You don't really have to do anything but watch him to be sure he's eating and don't let him choke."

"Okay, buddy," Joe said. "How about some spaghetti? What is this anyway?" he asked Marcie. "It smells terrific." He stuck a finger into the pasta to test the temperature, then licked off the sauce. "It *is* terrific."

"It's fettuccini Alfredo with chicken," she said. "He hasn't had it before."

Joe set the bowl down in front of Joshua and handed him his spoon. It took about ten minutes for Joshua to finish the pasta and drink some juice from a sippy cup, after which Marcie cleaned his hands and face and took him upstairs to bed. Joe walked up the stairs with them and watched as she got him settled in his crib and patted him while she sang a short lullaby.

The homey scene that played out in front of Joe almost choked him up. He'd never cried, even as a kid. He'd learned early that Kit, his mother, didn't have any sympathy or time for a crying child and so he'd learned to lock those feelings up inside him. He'd cried more since his son was born than he'd ever cried as a child. He'd shed tears of joy the night his son was born, tears of anguish when Joshua was stolen, and he'd had to accept that his child would never be found. And for some reason, he kept having to fight the stinging in his eyes tonight.

It was probably because it was the first chance he'd gotten to see how smart and adorable Joshua was, and how happy Marcie was, now that she had her baby back. He leaned against the door facing of the nursery and let himself soak in the poignant, precious scene before him.

Just as Marcie's lullaby was over and she'd slowed down on patting Joshua, he stirred and whimpered. He opened his eyes and looked at Marcie, then he started crying and wailing.

"Gram-m-ma," he sobbed. "Where Gramma?" His

crying got louder and louder. Marcie kept on patting his tummy as she tried to reassure him.

"Joshua, it's Mama, baby. It's Mama. You're okay, Shh, shh, baby."

With a squeezing in his chest that threatened to cut off his breath, Joe backed out of the room and went downstairs. He sat at the dining room table and picked up the glass of white wine he hadn't finished.

He swirled the liquid around, following the reflection of the chandelier, but soon he set the glass down. He didn't want more wine. Instead, he got up and took the plates to the kitchen, where he rinsed them and put them into the dishwasher. He put the leftover pasta into the refrigerator and wiped down the stove and counters.

Then he stepped out through the French doors onto the patio. It was pleasantly warm and he could smell the gardenias that Marcie loved so much. He stood looking up at the sky through damp, hazy eyes.

It was so easy for the therapists to talk about reintegration of the kidnapped child back into the family unit, about time frames and usual patterns. He couldn't count how many times he'd sat in his office listening to a psychologist or a social worker giving him progress reports on reunited families. But all of that had very little to do with reality. Reality was a scared little boy who had twice been yanked away from the people who loved him.

He'd only been nine months old when Rhoda had stolen him. It was doubtful that Joshua would ever have a conscious memory of those first months with Marcie and him. Then, twenty months later, he'd been ripped from the arms of the only parent he remembered. His *Gramma*. There was no question that Joshua was better off away from Howard, but would he ever fully recover from the loss of his Gramma? Would he learn to think of Marcie as his mother? And would he get the chance to know Joe, in his role of estranged husband and weekend dad?

Marcie opened the French doors and stepped out onto the patio. She closed the doors behind her and hooked the baby monitor onto her belt.

Joe's head angled slightly when he heard her but he didn't turn around. She stepped up beside him.

Still without looking at her, Joe asked, "So did you get him back to sleep?"

"Yes. It took a while. I've got the baby monitor in case he wakes up again."

"Does that happen often?"

Marcie gave a short, wry laugh. "In my vast experience of twelve days with my son? Yes. It happens every night."

Joe cleared his throat. "He'll get over it. He already calls you Mama."

"And you *Daddeee!*" she said, mimicking Joshua's enthusiastic inflection.

Joe nodded.

Marcie frowned, studying him. The way he wasn't looking at her. The slight hoarseness in his voice. "Is something wrong?" she asked. Then an awful thought hit her, right under her breastbone. "Has Child Services contacted you? Is it something about Joshua?"

He shook his head.

"Then what?" she asked, laying a hand on his arm.

He turned his head, looking down at her hand, then lifted his gaze to hers. "I'm just—" He shrugged and cleared his throat again. When he spoke, his voice was odd, as if he were fighting some strong emotion. "It's one of those days, I guess. Seeing him playing and eating and…"

"I know. It's a miracle, isn't it? That we have him back? Sometimes I just look at him and I start crying. He's so perfect. So beautiful." She took a shaky breath. "And then I get this awful, terrified feeling right here." She pressed her palm to the center of her chest. "And I cry some more, because I'm afraid they're going to take him away from me—" She stopped. "From us."

Joe drew in a swift breath, then whirled and walked away to the other edge of the patio. "You had it right the first time. *From you.*"

"I didn't mean that, Joe," she said quickly, moving to stand beside him again. "He's your son. I would never take that away from you."

He rubbed his forehead. "What would you do, Marcie? When can I expect you to start enforcing your never-want-to-see-you-again policy? Because right now I feel like I'm in a particularly hellish limbo. My son is back in my life—on alternate Tuesdays when you decide that it's a convenient night for me to drop by in time to see him falling asleep. Thanks, by the way, for the half hour of playtime and feeding tonight."

His voice was so bitter, so angry, it took Marcie aback, and she realized that she had been so caught up in the all-day, every-day life of a mom and the miracle of having her child back, even if he didn't quite know who she was yet, that she'd completely neglected and ignored Joe's feelings.

She also realized that the question she'd been planning to ask him tonight wasn't going to happen. Her plan—her fantasy—had been that the two of them would come out onto the patio after dinner and have a pleasant, meaningful conversation about where their lives were going from here. They'd talk about being together for their child and Joe might say something about how expensive his apartment was, which would give Marcie the opening to suggest that he move back into the house.

But instead of being excited about how smart Joshua was and how cool it was to watch him feed himself, Joe had become angry.

"I'm sorry, Joe. I've handled all this badly."

He turned to face her. "No, you haven't. You're a wonderful mom. It's obvious Joshua already loves you."

She shook her head. "He loves *Gramma* and he thinks you are the best thing ever, *Daddeee!* To him, I'm just the nanny." To her dismay, her voice broke.

"You don't see it, but I do. He couldn't take his eyes off you while we were putting the square box in the triangular hole. He wanted you to see everything."

Marcie felt the breeze cool on her cheeks as it dried her tears. "I nearly went crazy when he was stolen." She chuckled wryly. "I know, understatement of the year. I know I blamed you. I know I was mean to you and I completely ignored that you had lost a child, too. I was too sad and too broken to realize that I was destroying the only person who could help me.

"Marcie—"

"Let me finish. I know now that you had to leave or I would have totally destroyed you. As it is I've said things that I know you can never forgive. But, Joe, if you could try. If you could possibly forgive me—"

"Okay, that's enough," Joe snapped. "What is this? Did the social worker tell you it's time to mend fences? Well, it's not going to work. You forget that in my job I hear all this. The psychologists and social workers report to me, so I know that this is just about the time in the reintegration process where the parent is told to make amends."

"That's not—"

"Come on, Marc—"

"I love you!" Marcie shouted because that was the only way she could think of to stop him. "I love you and I want you here, with Joshua and me. Is that *amends* enough for you?"

For a second, Joe stared at her with his mouth open. In his eyes she could see a faint spark of hope. But in the next second he'd thrown up that armor he'd developed as a child growing up in strip clubs and never knowing who was going to be taking care of him. "Don't, Marcie. Just don—"

She propelled herself at him and hit her target—his mouth with her lips. It looked like the only way she was going to knock him out of his cynical, disbelieving attitude, was to kiss it out of him. And if that didn't work, if she couldn't seduce her own husband, then she'd have to admit defeat.

At first, his lips didn't move. But he was affected. It didn't take her long to notice that he was becoming turned on. She kept on kissing him, using her tongue as she tried to tease his lips apart. She felt like a victorious warrior when he relented and she was able to explore the inside of his mouth. But then he lifted his head to look down at her and she felt her stomach drop to her toes. Was he going to stop her?

He didn't. What he did was pull her up against him and bend her head back and kiss her until she felt faint. Then he kissed her some more. Hard and deep and sensual. This was a promise and a threat, an awakening and an ending. It was overtly sexual and by the time it ended, Marcie's lungs were heaving with reaction and her body, all the way down to its core, was screaming for release.

Joe stopped suddenly, his own chest heaving, and eyed her as if she were some alien siren. "What are you doing?" he gasped.

"Trying to shut you up," she responded breathily.

"Shut me up?"

She nodded, feeling the tears begin to gather in her eyes. "Oh, I am so tired of crying," she muttered. "I was trying to say something, but you kept interrupting me."

He pressed his lips together. "Okay. Say what you wanted to say."

"Joe, I love you. I always have. Can you please forgive me? If not for me, for the sake of our baby? Joshua needs you, and not just on the days I can work up enough nerve to ask you to come over. He needs you every day, and so do I. I promise you that I will earn your trust again." She'd done it. She'd said her piece as simply and clearly as she could. Now it was up to him.

He didn't find it easy to trust, she knew. Especially women. His mother had seen to that. Marcie had fought for years to prove he could trust her, and then, after Joshua was taken, she'd proven to him that he couldn't. Now she had to start over.

As she watched, his mouth relaxed and the frown lines between his brows smoothed out. Her pulse pounded as she waited to hear what he was going to say.

"Marcie, I—" He took a breath. "You have my trust. And my heart. I want us to be a family again. I want us to be three again."

"Oh," Marcie said, noticing that tears were streaming down her cheeks again. "Hold me, Joe, and never, ever let me go."

Joe pulled her close and she tucked her head into her favorite place, the little hollow between his shoulder and head. He pressed his cheek against her hair. They stood that way for a long time. Finally, Joe took Marcie's hand and led her into the house and up the stairs to their bedroom.

Quite a while later, the two of them lay languid and satiated, on the bed in the master bedroom. Joe tightened his arm around Marcie and kissed the top of her head. "I love you, Marcie," he whispered.

She nodded. "I love you, too," she said in a small voice. "I never thought we'd be together again. I thought I'd lost my baby and my husband."

"Well, you haven't," Joe said. He pushed up in the bed and leaned back against the headboard, pulling Marcie with him. "And you never will again. Joshua and I are right here and we always will be. We're a family," he said. "We are three."

Marcie looked up at her husband. "You know what I'd like?" she asked.

He smiled down at her. "Tell me," he said.

"I'd like it if we were four."

Joe's smile widened into a huge grin. "You would?"

She bit her lip as she nodded. Her eyes sparkled like diamonds. "Want to start now?"

Joe bent his head and caught her mouth in a long, deep kiss. "Absolutely," he muttered.

* * * * *

Look for more exciting books in Mallory Kane's miniseries, THE DELANCEY DYNASTY, *later in 2014. You'll find them wherever Harlequin Intrigue books are sold!*

COMING NEXT MONTH FROM

HARLEQUIN®

INTRIGUE®

Available January 21, 2014

#1473 BLOOD ON COPPERHEAD TRAIL
Bitterwood P.D.
Paula Graves
Laney Hanvey's job fighting corruption pits her against police chief
Doyle Massey, but they must work together when three girls disappear.

#1474 UNDERCOVER CAPTOR
Shadow Agents: Guts and Glory
Cynthia Eden
When Dr. Tina Jamison is kidnapped by a group determined to destroy
the EOD, her only hope of survival rests with dangerous undercover agent
Drew Lancaster.

#1475 ROCKY MOUNTAIN REVENGE
Cindi Myers
FBI agent Jacob Westmoreland tracks down his former flame,
Elizabeth Giardino, in order to bring one man to justice: her father.

#1476 TENNESSEE TAKEDOWN
Lena Diaz
Caught at the wrong place at the wrong time, an accountant must rely
upon a hunky SWAT detective as she runs for her life.

#1477 RANCHER RESCUE
Barb Han
A cowboy comes to Katherine Harper's aid only to find himself the new
target of a man who will stop at nothing to silence them both.

#1478 RAVEN'S HOLLOW
Jenna Ryan
Eli Blume and Sadie Bellam meet again in a haunted hollow,
where someone hungering for revenge lurks in the shadows.

HICNM0114

REQUEST YOUR FREE BOOKS!
2 FREE NOVELS PLUS 2 FREE GIFTS!

HARLEQUIN®

INTRIGUE®

BREATHTAKING ROMANTIC SUSPENSE

YES! Please send me 2 FREE Harlequin Intrigue® novels and my 2 FREE gifts (gifts are worth about $10). After receiving them, if I don't wish to receive any more books, I can return the shipping statement marked "cancel." If I don't cancel, I will receive 6 brand-new novels every month and be billed just $4.74 per book in the U.S. or $5.24 per book in Canada. That's a savings of at least 14% off the cover price! It's quite a bargain! Shipping and handling is just 50¢ per book in the U.S. and 75¢ per book in Canada.* I understand that accepting the 2 free books and gifts places me under no obligation to buy anything. I can always return a shipment and cancel at any time. Even if I never buy another book, the two free books and gifts are mine to keep forever.

182/382 HDN F42N

Name _____ (PLEASE PRINT) _____

Address _____ Apt. # _____

City _____ State/Prov. _____ Zip/Postal Code _____

Signature (if under 18, a parent or guardian must sign) _____

Mail to the **Harlequin® Reader Service:**
IN U.S.A.: P.O. Box 1867, Buffalo, NY 14240-1867
IN CANADA: P.O. Box 609, Fort Erie, Ontario L2A 5X3
**Are you a subscriber to Harlequin Intrigue books
and want to receive the larger-print edition?
Call 1-800-873-8635 or visit www.ReaderService.com.**

* Terms and prices subject to change without notice. Prices do not include applicable taxes. Sales tax applicable in N.Y. Canadian residents will be charged applicable taxes. Offer not valid in Quebec. This offer is limited to one order per household. Not valid for current subscribers to Harlequin Intrigue books. All orders subject to credit approval. Credit or debit balances in a customer's account(s) may be offset by any other outstanding balance owed by or to the customer. Please allow 4 to 6 weeks for delivery. Offer available while quantities last.

Your Privacy—The Harlequin® Reader Service is committed to protecting your privacy. Our Privacy Policy is available online at www.ReaderService.com or upon request from the Harlequin Reader Service.

We make a portion of our mailing list available to reputable third parties that offer products we believe may interest you. If you prefer that we not exchange your name with third parties, or if you wish to clarify or modify your communication preferences, please visit us at www.ReaderService.com/consumerschoice or write to us at Harlequin Reader Service Preference Service, P.O. Box 9062, Buffalo, NY 14269. Include your complete name and address.

HI13R

BLOOD ON COPPERHEAD TRAIL
by Paula Graves

Nothing can stop Laney Hanvey from looking for her missing sister. Not even sexy new chief of Bitterwood P.D....

"I'm not going to be handled out of looking for my sister," Laney growled as she heard footsteps catching up behind her on the hiking trail.

"I'm just here to help."

She faltered to a stop, turning to look at Doyle Massey. He wasn't exactly struggling to keep up with her—life on the beach had clearly kept him in pretty good shape. But he was out of his element.

She'd grown up in these mountains. Her mother had always joked she was half mountain goat, half Indian scout. She knew these hills as well as she knew her own soul. "You'll slow me down."

"Maybe that's a good thing."

She glared at him, her rising terror looking for a target. "My sister is out here somewhere and I'm going to find her."

The look Doyle gave her was full of pity. The urge to slap that expression off his face was so strong she had to clench her hands. "You're rushing off alone into the woods where a man with a gun has just committed a murder."

"A gun?" She couldn't stop her gaze from slanting toward the crime scene. "She was shot?"

"Two rounds to the back of the head."

HIEXP69740

She closed her eyes, the remains of the cucumber sandwich she'd eaten at Sequoyah House rising in her throat. She stumbled a few feet away from Doyle Massey and gave up fighting the nausea.

After her stomach was empty, she crouched in the underbrush, fighting dry heaves and giving in to the hot tears burning her eyes. The heat of Massey's hand on her back was comforting, even though she was embarrassed by her display.

"I will help you search," he said in a low, gentle tone. "But I want you to take a minute to just breathe and think. Okay? I want you to think about your sister and where you think she'd go. Do you know?"

Does Laney hold the key to her sister's whereabouts?
Doyle Massey intends to find out, in Paula Graves's
BLOOD ON COPPERHEAD TRAIL,
on sale in February 2014!

HARLEQUIN®

INTRIGUE®

ATTEMPTING THE IMPOSSIBLE

Despite her new identity in the WitSec program,
Ann Gardiner has been found by the one person who
hurt her the most: FBI agent Jake Westmoreland. The lying
SOB slept with her to get access to her father. And when
she testified against her own flesh and blood, her whole
existence was turned upside down. Jake couldn't expect
any more from her—except that he did. He wanted the
impossible—her help.

Jake doesn't have much time to restore Ann's faith in him,
but she is the only one who can help him locate her mob
boss father and put him away for good.

ROCKY MOUNTAIN REVENGE

BY CINDI MYERS

Available February 2014, only from Harlequin® Intrigue®.

HI69742